DOWN & DIRTY

MOSH SERIES BOOK 2

SUSANNA ROGERS

Bucher & Reid

Bucher & Reid

Cover by Amygdala Book Design
978-0-6484920-2-3

ALSO BY SUSANNA ROGERS

CHAPTER ONE

Austin

Coming home was supposed to be a beautiful thing but after being away for so long I wasn't sure where I belonged anymore.

Still, one thing was for certain. Being back in Frankston beat the hell out of back-to-back tours and being on the road constantly. Or in the private jet. Not that any of us actually owned our own aircraft but none of us was going to say no to hiring one and, hey, it was such a practical means of transport.

That was how crazy our lives had become. It didn't seem real. Sometimes it felt as if I'd walked into someone else's life by accident.

And now we were at The Swamp, which was like turning the clock back to the beginning, the first gigs, the grungy music, the dive bars. The place was a dump but at least it wasn't pretending to be something it wasn't, and the beer was cold. Or at least I hoped it was.

Such a relief to be able to hang back and gaze at the crowd instead of being the guy everyone was looking at on stage. How did Nick even know all these people? He probably didn't.

"Oh my god, you're Austin Murphy!"

So much for not being recognized. "Yep, that's me."

Two wide-eyed girls giggled and asked for a photo. It only took a moment to help them out and it made their day so I was happy to go along with it, but they looked so young that they made me feel ancient. Not that thirty was old. It was just the beginning, maybe a new beginning.

That decided it. I needed a drink so I edged my way closer to the bar. Didn't quite make it. The bartender handed across a cocktail, that was all she did, yet she looked like she'd been transported from a 1950s Hollywood film set, the starlet waiting to be discovered. How could I not have noticed her earlier?

It wasn't the red lipstick and blue eyes lined with black, or the jet black hair with the purple streak, or the polka dot shirt tied at the waist that had rockabilly written all over it that grabbed me. It was the confidence in her movements, the fire in her eyes, the personality in her face.

And maybe, just a little, it was those boobs in the push-up bra. My mouth dry, I swallowed. Yep, definitely the boobs.

Wiping the sweat from my forehead, I realized she was serving Nick and Lily. Giving Nick a serve too, by the look of it, which only made me like this woman more. Then she was onto the next customer, smiling, making eye contact, shaking up the next cocktail. She wasn't just a bartender. She looked like she owned the place, which was a lot more than I could say for Nick, who was most likely in full-on drinking mode.

Now I needed a beer more than ever but I had to get my shit together before I went up to the bar or I was going to look like a total jerk. Just two minutes, that was all I'd need.

Turning away, I tried not to stare. And failed.

Then Lachie came my way, gave me a fist bump. "Man, I love this place."

I glanced at the bar or, rather, the bartender. "I'm loving it too."

"Look at all this talent. We're surrounded by fans, girls, pretty young things who want us."

I held a hand out, as if pushing them away. "That's not for me."

Lachie made out like he was a party animal. And he was. But underneath, there was a big kid who'd insisted on coming back home so he could help take care of his dad. He had a huge heart even if he didn't want anyone to see it.

"And it's all free," he added. "Free beer, free booze, whatever we want."

"It's not free. Nick's paying."

He brushed it off and knocked back some more beer.

I'd been through this with him before. Nothing was free in this business. Anything the record company spent got charged back to us, as we'd found out early in the game. When we'd first started we were like little kids, excited about the limo greeting us at the airport, the bottles of Bolly, the huge parties the label put on, the hot shots who charged for the pleasure of their presence—until we realized we were paying for it all.

"Gotta make sure Nick has plenty to drink too," Lachie said. "Maybe even a little drinking competition."

I glanced at Lily through the crowd. "Give him a break."

"What? He's the one who's put on the party."

"All I'm saying is just let things take their own course. It's not like he needs any encouragement."

And neither do you. Suddenly I felt like a sad ass aging rock star. Yet another reason I didn't quite fit with the guys.

I glanced at the bartender and felt a surge of energy. That was more like it.

Lachie looked around, frowning. "What's this shit they're playing?"

I raised my eyebrows. "That 'shit' would be Elvis." He didn't say anything so I added, "From the Sun Sessions."

Definitely not Nick's choice of music. The other guys loved my bass playing, and they appreciated what I brought to the table, the way I could boogie over a shuffle all day long, but they weren't into rockabilly and old style rock 'n' roll the way I was.

Lachie leaned closer. "Can I get you a drink?"

"I'm good, thanks."

A small lie because I was getting that drink myself, and I'd already spent way too much time with Lachie when I had other things in mind. He was so drunk he probably hadn't seen me eying up the bartender. Probably just as well. Then he was off.

I didn't even know why I was talking to Lachie when I should be getting closer to the babe behind the bar. Only one thing stood between me and her, or maybe two things, Nick and Lily.

It would've been rude not to greet Nick. It was his bar, his party, and he was the one I was going to let down when he found out what was coming. My throat tight, I swallowed, trying to act like everything was fine.

I gave Lily a hug. She was a petite little thing, especially when she was next to Nick, and there was always something that made me feel for her, even if I couldn't work out what it was.

I asked about their son because he was a cute kid. Also I didn't think the other guys quite got what it meant to have a child of your own. Not that I did, but I tried to put myself in other people's shoes sometimes.

Like Nick, for instance. He wasn't the world's best partner to Lily, not her partner at all in fact, but he'd always done his bit as a father and he was overjoyed to be back with his boy. You could see it in his eyes.

I glanced at the bar, pretended I wasn't staring, and tried to look suave in case the bartender looked my way. She didn't. Somehow I ended up feeling more like a bumbling schoolboy than a famous musician. Not that 'famous' was important to me but that woman might be.

I turned to Nick. "I can't believe you bought The Swamp. Man, this brings back memories."

"Sure does," he said.

Problem was, his memories were completely different from mine even though we played the same gigs to the same crowds, most of them anyway. He and Lachie went back further than The Merchants. They'd always been tight. Meanwhile, Cooper had gone to school with them and was the best rock 'n' roll drummer around, in my humble opinion.

And then there was me. Even four years down the track, I was still the new guy.

I got that strange sensation of being alone in a room full of people, of being the odd one out, a feeling I got a lot despite the fact these guys were my friends and they were good people.

They might not be so friendly when they found out what was coming their way, though. It made my gut clench, made me feel like even more of an outsider. Still, I couldn't say anything tonight, as much as I wanted to get it over and done with.

I'd always got on well with Lily because in some ways she was older than the other guys in the band, not in years, but she'd had to grow up quickly after getting pregnant. Maybe that made her different.

Leaning over, I whispered in her ear, "Do you ever feel out of place?"

She chuckled. "All the time!"

I laughed too. Because it was better than crying. Besides, I reveled in the things that made me different, my individuality and my distinct tastes and experiences, even if they were the very things that singled me out.

Still smiling, Lily gazed longingly at Nick who wasn't even looking her way. That was when it hit me like a baseball bat, so clear I didn't know why I hadn't seen it before. She was still into him. Big time. Maybe even still in love.

Man, I felt for her because Nick's head was somewhere else. His dick had been a lot of other places too, not that I was much better. Until recently when I decided I'd had enough of all that rock star bullshit. Because that's exactly what it was. A load of crap.

I wished I could help Lily but this was so far out of my league it wasn't funny and I had enough problems of my own.

I told the two of them I'd join them in the band room, then turned to the bar and got a glimpse of that amazing bartender, a jolt rocketing through my whole body. And I mean, my *whole* body. I tried to shake it off and suck some air in.

Miss Rockabilly Bartender caught my eye as I leaned against the bar, acknowledged me with a nod, and kept serving her current customers. I had to admire her professional approach. In fact, there was a lot to admire as she leaned forward to listen to them place their order. It was getting kind of noisy in here, not necessarily a bad thing. Maybe I'd have to get close too so she could hear me.

She came over as soon as she was done with them. "What can I get you?"

"Beer, thanks."

"What kind?"

"What would you recommend?" Hopefully I sounded more like James Bond than Homer Simpson.

She stepped to one side so I could see behind her. "We've got a range of beers in the fridge and a couple on tap."

But I wasn't looking at the beer selection, my eyes glued to the fabulous figure in front of me. This woman was all curves. I swallowed, deciding I'd go for something on tap. It'd take longer.

I pointed to the beer tap. "What's this one?"

"That's our Frankston IPA made right here in town."

I smiled. "Pale ale. Gotta be good if it's local."

She placed her hand on the tap and started pouring. Her hands looked very soft for a barmaid, her arms smooth and pale. I had to stop myself from reaching out and touching to see if she was real.

I took the beer from her. "Are you from around

here?"

This was a big town, a city really, with a small rockabilly scene, only I hadn't seen her around, which seemed unusual.

"I'm not from Nevada." She tilted her head. "I'm from all over the place."

"Intriguing."

"Believe me, it's not as exciting as it sounds."

"Have you worked here long?"

"Longer than your friend has owned the place."

I opened my mouth to speak. Of course, she knew I played in the band with Nick.

"Everyone knows who you are," she added.

"Not everyone. Bet your grandmother doesn't know."

She shrugged one pretty shoulder. "She doesn't know much anymore. She passed away a couple of years ago."

"I'm sorry."

"You're right, though. She used to listen to Frank Sinatra and Pat Boone. On a good day she might stretch to Barry Manilow, nothing heavier than that."

I sipped my beer. "So you didn't get your taste from her?"

She tossed her head back. "What makes you think I'm not a Manilow fan?"

"Elvis was playing earlier. Now it's Johnny Cash. My guess is you chose the music for tonight because Nick sure as hell didn't."

She smiled, gazed at me with those mesmerizing blue eyes, gave me her full attention. I could have stayed like this all night. In fact, I was thinking she could hold a lot more than my attention. There was one body part of mine in particular that she could hold all night long.

I gulped back some beer so I could settle down a bit because I wasn't going to make a good impression acting like a randy teenager.

"You remind me of a song," she said.

"Really?"

"*One of these things.*"

"Can't say I've heard it."

She leaned closer so I got a glimpse of creamy cleavage. "You've seen Sesame Street, haven't you? You must know the song where they show three red balloons and one blue and you're supposed to identify the item that doesn't belong." She hummed the tune.

"And I'm the blue balloon?"

She gave a long, slow nod.

"Ha! You've got that right."

How amazing that she'd known me for all of five minutes and she'd nailed it. It made me feel there was hope after all. The other guys didn't get it, didn't know how it felt to be an outsider, to be part of something and never really quite there.

"Looks like your other friend needs a drink," she said.

Lachie was leaning across the bar. She excused herself and served him, getting back to work.

Meanwhile, I hadn't even gotten her name. What the hell was I thinking? I hung near the bar, hoping she'd come closer but some guy started tending bar near me instead while she was busy at the other end.

I wasn't done yet, though, nowhere near it.

Strange sounds started coming from the band room, loud thumps followed by whoops and laughter. I looked around. Lachie wasn't here anymore and Nick had said he was going to the band room. It was never good when those two got together, not when they were both tanked up.

I drummed my fingers on the bar. I should go in there and break it up, whatever the hell it was those two were up to, and then I'd feel like a granddad again. Letting out a long sigh, I got up.

I only made it as far as the doorway when I saw bits of broken furniture on the stage at the far end, parachuting ripped down from the ceiling. It had Nick and Lachie's name written all over it. This was exactly the sort of stupid thing they'd do when they were drunk.

Lachie was on stage, lifting a chair ready to smash it, Nick beside him. Miss Rockabilly was there too, giving him a big shove. Nick stumbled, looked like a little kid about to get told off by the kindergarten teacher.

I couldn't hear what she said but it must've been good because Lachie was doubled over with laughter while she ushered Nick from the stage. That was the thing with Nick. Sometimes he needed a monumental kick up the butt before he'd pay attention, not that she was humiliating him, just putting a stop to his antics.

Now that the commotion was over, she yelled, "Come on, guys, there's plenty of drinks at the bar."

I'm not sure what it was—the way she took control, her refusal to let anyone push her around, or maybe it was still down to those boobs busting out of that top—but that decided it for me.

The woman was a firecracker.

And I needed a little explosion in my life.

CHAPTER TWO

Tara

I should've been relieved it was closing time. Instead my chest was heaving, my blood pressure rising because I was worried I'd gone too far this time.

I hadn't been able to help it. It wasn't just tonight. It was everything. Then seeing Nick and Lachie trash the place was the last straw. Those guys had so much money they didn't know what to do with it, didn't know what life was like for other people, or maybe they'd forgotten.

Besides which, Nick had no idea about running a bar. Sure, he was refurbishing The Swamp but if there was nothing left of it until after the renovations were completed, I wouldn't have a place to work in the meantime. And I needed to work, something a guy like him was never going to understand.

I'd already wiped down the bar and was putting the chairs upside down on the tables so the cleaners would be able to sweep and mop in the morning. I'd known tonight was going to be messy, even if I hadn't foreseen quite how bad, and now we had to get the place in order for the Thursday lunch rush because, for some reason, that was the one part of the market that the previous owner had nailed.

Eliza was in the back recuperating. Honestly, I could kill that girl, tonight of all nights, the first night the new owner was back in town. I'd already told her to stay put and not let anyone see her. I even used the words, "Don't move," which was a pretty stupid thing to say to a teenage girl who was legless and clearly wasn't going anywhere on her own.

The other bar staff understood and were helping to cover my ass tonight, because the last thing I needed was an excuse for the owner to fire me. Even an owner as inexperienced as Nick knew how much trouble he could get into if he was caught with underage drinkers in the bar, not to mention he might not be so understanding after my little performance tonight.

Spinning around in a hurry, I crashed into Austin Murphy, our chests colliding. Embarrassing to say the least because hardly anyone else was around and it wasn't as if there were a lot of things to crash into around here.

His hands on my shoulders, he held me in place so I didn't topple over, his body strong against mine, so hard he made me feel secure and safe. A second later, I had my head together as he gave me some space.

"I thought you would've gone home already." That was the first thing that came out of my mouth. Maybe I wasn't as 'together' as I thought.

He didn't seem perturbed in the slightest. In fact, he looked like he was enjoying this way too much. Also, if I'd felt the hardness of his chest, no doubt he'd felt my boobs. They were hard to miss, which was not his fault. Not my fault the damn things were so big either.

I took a deep breath because I had to control that temper of mine. I'd already done enough damage tonight and the last thing I needed was to rub the boss's close friend up the wrong way.

"Sorry," I said. "I didn't mean it that way. It's just… It's late, you know."

"Sure." He nodded toward the entry. "I was hanging around talking to Nick after everyone left and now the front doors are locked."

"I noticed." Of course I'd noticed him. How could I not have noticed him? And how could I keep putting my foot in my mouth? "Not you. I mean, the guys always lock the front door so we don't get any strays coming in." I held a hand out. "Not that you're a stray. That's not what I meant either."

"No, tonight I'm a hanger on."

I looked around. "So Nick's gone already?"

"Yep, he and Lachie are going to finish themselves off at Nick's."

"Not you?"

He smiled. "Not my style."

I stepped away. "Then I'll show you the way. To the back door, that is."

He touched my arm, sent a sizzle up my spine, and no wonder. This guy was the whole package. It wasn't just the 1950s movie star looks, the dark hair slicked back into a slightly messy quiff or the equally dark eyes or pointed sideburns.

No, I shouldn't go there. I took a deep breath instead. He was just a guy and I wasn't impressed by fame and stardom and everything that went with it. Those things didn't mean he was a good person, especially not if Nick was anything to go by, and I had bigger things to worry about tonight.

"I didn't catch your name," he said.

"Tara."

I slowed down to his pace as we ambled toward the back of the bar. Normally at this time of night, I'd be racing around like a crazy woman but right now the only thing that was racing was my pulse.

"Do you have a last name or are you one of those people like Cher or Madonna who only have one name?"

"Tara Coleman." I shrugged. "If I was wealthy and famous like Madonna I wouldn't be cleaning up after closing."

"Is there anything I can help you with, Tara?"

"What? Like taking out the trash?" I laughed, couldn't help myself, because the mental image of the rich rock star doing something so menial was too much for me. Or maybe I was simply too tired.

"Sure," he said, like it was nothing.

But it wasn't nothing. I needed to get him through the back exit. Had to hope the door to the staff room was closed so he didn't see Eliza flaked out in there or I'd have way too much explaining to do.

"Already done," I said. "I'll just let you out."

I stopped by the fire door that led out back and scanned the entire bar, out of habit more than anything.

"I should stay and make sure you're safe," Austin said.

Stay? No way. He should get out of here quickly and smoothly so I could deal with my little sister.

The look on my face must've been dire because he held a hand out. "Not that I think you need saving or anything. It's just common sense for you to have someone with you when you're leaving late at night and there's no one else around."

"Just a sec." I switched off the lights, then pulled the door open. "There's someone around all right." I pointed down the short hallway where one of the bouncers was on his phone, waiting for me. Though he didn't look threatening right now, he had a face that could change from friendly to forceful in an instant.

"Austin, this is Tyrone," I said.

"Pleased to meet you." Tyrone grinned like crazy because clearly the novelty of being surrounded by rock stars all night hadn't faded.

"Likewise." Austin shook his hand.

While Tyrone had him distracted, I slid across and closed the door to the staff area so you couldn't see inside.

Tyrone looked at me. "Nearly ready?"

Austin sidled closer. "Sure you don't need a hand?"

"No, we'll be—" Tyrone began.

"We'll be fine." I jumped in quickly and tried to signal Tyrone with my eyes because I didn't need Austin hanging around when my sister was in a drunken stupor in the next room.

Tyrone nodded.

"Sure." Austin frowned, didn't argue.

A huge thump thudded through the air, clearly coming from the back room, and I had a terrible feeling I knew what'd just happened. My stomach sank.

"What was that?" Austin said.

I took his arm to lead him away. "Nothing."

This was followed by a loud moan. I cringed.

He turned to Tyrone. "Doesn't sound like nothing." Then he looked at me. "Is everything all right?"

"Taaaara." Eliza's voice.

I pressed my eyes shut for a moment. "Yep, it's all fine."

"TAAAARA." Louder this time.

There was no hiding this any longer. Sighing, I pushed open the door to the back room where, sure enough, my sister had fallen off the chair where we'd propped her up in the corner, landing on the floor with her skinny legs splayed. Not a good look when she was wearing such a short skirt. Aside from that, her hair was a mess, eyeliner was running down her face, and her lipstick had been smudged off ages ago.

Slipping my hands under her arms, I lifted her back onto the chair. "We've got to get you home, honey."

Her eyes stayed closed, a low rumble escaping her lips.

Austin raised his eyebrows. "Home?"

"Meet Eliza. My sister."

He looked down, then did a double-take. "Hey, I know her."

"You do?"

"She and her friend asked me for a photo earlier on. They seemed kinda funny, giggled a lot. I didn't realize how young they were."

I heard the shock in his voice. Disapproval even. It was nothing compared to how mad I was when I'd found Eliza earlier tonight, but I'd calmed down since then. The bar had been too damned busy, for one thing.

"Yeah, she looks a lot younger now her makeup has come off," I said in a small voice.

"How old, exactly?"

I could lie but didn't. "Sixteen."

He glanced back at Tyrone, then at me. "Who let her

in?"

"No one." I jumped in because this was absolutely not Tyrone's fault. "Eliza snuck in through the back with a friend. She knew the way in. Believe me, no way could she have gotten past Tyrone or any of the guys at the door."

"How'd she get hold of the booze? Surely she didn't get served at the bar."

I shook my head. "None of us would have served her. The girls grabbed a bottle of Southern Comfort to share. Knew where to find that too. They stayed away from me all night and the place was so crowded I didn't notice they were here until it was too late."

Austin frowned, his expression hardening, the look on his face somewhere between dire and concerned. My heart pounded in my chest while I hoped like hell he wasn't going to mention this to my new boss.

Eliza worried me too. She didn't have anyone else. There was only me. I had to take care of her and wasn't exactly doing a stellar job despite my best efforts. Besides, I couldn't provide for her if I didn't have a job. I'd already lost my last bar job when the place closed down thanks to a drunken owner.

I gritted my teeth. "That Michaela…"

"Who?"

"Eliza's friend." I pressed a hand to my temple. "Sorry, I'm not making excuses for Eliza but this escapade has her best friend's name written all over it. Eliza's just as bad. She's the one who brought their little plan to life."

Despite this, the person I was angriest at was Michaela's mother. She'd come to pick her daughter up after my frantic phone call and had refused to take Eliza with them. Hadn't cared what might happen to her or that

I was working. All because she thought Eliza was a bad influence on her little darling who would never have done something like this on her own.

I could throttle 'her little darling'. I could throttle both of them, Michaela's mother too. Not that I'd ever lay a hand on Eliza, even when she did her best to drive me to it. My heart rate rose all over again.

Austin crouched in front of her. "How much has she had to drink?"

"There wasn't much left in the bottle after the two of them got to it. Don't know if they've had anything else."

He touched her cheeks gently, making her eyes open. She whacked his hand away. "Hey, y-you're from the b-band." Slurring her words but at least she could speak.

"Yep, I'm Austin." He stood. "She won't need a doctor, just a good night's sleep. This'll make for one hell of a hangover. I'll help you get her to the car."

"Need a hand?" Tyrone asked.

"I've got her." Austin swept Eliza up into his arms as if she didn't weigh a thing and maybe, just maybe, he swept up a little piece of my heart at the same time. "Can you get the door?"

"Sure thing." Tyrone stepped back to hold the back door open while I grabbed my purse and slung it over my shoulder, grateful I had not one but two guys to help me out tonight. Sometimes it was a relief not to feel like I was on my own all the time.

After we made it outside, Tyrone locked the back door behind us and I breathed another sigh of relief, the night air refreshing. More than refreshing actually, and I hoped it might knock some sense into my sister.

Eliza started wriggling and moaning about something,

so Austin lowered her to her feet.

"Are you okay to stand?" he asked.

She nuzzled into his chest. "Of course I can stand."

To my amazement, she sounded almost coherent.

"Do you think you can walk a few steps?" he asked.

Her face was still stuck in his chest "I can walk. I'm not a baby."

Not much, you're not. I bit my lip to stop myself from saying this because it'd only make things worse.

"Is there anything I can do?" Tyrone asked.

"We've got this under control." Austin turned to me. "I'll help get her into your car. Is that okay with you?"

I nodded. "Tyrone, you should get going."

He had a toddler at home who didn't understand Daddy worked until the early hours of the morning, and then sometimes woke him earlier than he'd like.

I had a family too. Eliza was it, and right now she was a mammoth pain in the neck.

Tyrone got into his truck and drove off while Eliza was still hanging off Austin.

Sometimes I wished I had her life. Wished *I* was the one who had someone to take care of me. I even wished I was the one draped across Austin's chest. That wouldn't be such a bad place to be, not bad at all.

I sucked in a deep breath because I still had to get Eliza home and then tomorrow I'd have to give her a big talking to. My heart sank. I wanted to be a mom one day, truly I did, but I hadn't signed up for this. At twenty-four, I was nowhere near old enough to be the mother of a sixteen-year-old, yet there were plenty of times I had to be mother and big sister all rolled into one.

Eliza stood on the spot, swaying. "I can walk."

"If you want to walk, that's fine," Austin said. "We'll take it nice and slow." Then to me. "Is that your car?" He pointed to the Micra, old but reliable.

"Yep."

Eliza leaned onto his chest again. "You're nice."

"Um, thanks." He kept his arm around her.

"I said to Mic... Mic..."

"Michaela."

Eliza nodded. "I said to her I don't care if you're only the bass player. Y-you seem nice anyway."

I covered my mouth to stifle a giggle.

My little sister continued in slobbering idiot mode. "We got photos with Nick Steel and Lachie Tyler too. The girls at school will be sooo jealous."

"Great," Austin said.

"Tara says Nick is—"

I jumped in. "Honey, we've got to get you to the car."

"Car, schmar." Slurring her words now. "All the girls love Nick and Lachie. They're famous." She rolled her head around. "Always Nick and Lachie."

"Eliza, listen to me." Austin tightened his grip, holding her up. Her head landed back on his chest again. "Nick and Lachie are nice guys but just because they play in a band doesn't mean you should go chasing after them. You've had way too much to drink. It's lucky for you Tara is here. I'm here too."

She hiccupped, her skinny little body shaking. Panic shot through me. I couldn't see her face, probably turning green. Oh, hell, I knew what was coming and reached for her shoulders, ready to pull her away.

Too slow. A second too slow.

My little sister convulsed, her whole body undulating,

as she threw up the contents of her stomach down the front of Austin Murphy's shirt. My hand flew to my mouth.

"I'm so sorry!" I yelled. "Eliza, are you okay?"

She nuzzled her head against Austin and moaned. I moaned too. Couldn't help it.

Austin raised his eyebrows, looked at me. My mortification was reaching new heights or, rather, depths.

"Feel better now?" he asked her.

She nodded, kept nuzzling into his shirt.

"Oh, honey." Despair in my voice as I turned to Austin. "I'm so sorry."

"You already said that. It's fine."

My stomach sank and swam at the same time, and not just because of the stench. What a guy. He must've been grossed out, must want to dump the poor girl, must want to clean himself up too. Most people would have lost their shit by now. Not him.

"Okay," he said. "I guess she's not walking after all."

My hands shook as I reached for Eliza. "M-maybe if you can just help me get her into the car."

"I've got her."

He ignored Eliza's protests and swept her right back up into his arms. I hoped at the very least that she felt better after depositing a bucket load of vomit over the man who was trying to help her because she was going to feel diabolical tomorrow.

I pulled open the passenger door and Austin slid Eliza onto the front seat where she flopped into a heap. At least she could keep her head up now.

"I'll get your seat belt." He reached across and secured her in place, then draped his arm over the open door and looked at me.

I bit my lip, not sure what to say because I had no idea of the protocols for this sort of situation. Was there even an accepted etiquette for the correct thing to do after your little sister has vomited on your new boss's friend?

"I'd better wipe her mouth," I said in a small voice.

"No, she's fine. She wiped most of it off onto my shirt."

"Oh, no, I'm so—"

Austin held a hand out. "I know. You're sorry. It's okay, really. She's young. She made a mistake. We've all done stupid things when we were young."

He was right and didn't I know it.

I nodded. "Thanks so much for all your help. I'll take her home now."

"I'll come with you."

"That's kind but you've done so much already."

"It's not a problem."

"Then how will you get home? You'll need a ride back to your car after I put Eliza to bed." I frowned, looked around the small parking lot. "Where is your car?"

"The Thunderbird's parked out on the street."

That figured. My dream car, the only vehicle that could make me weak at the knees. And I'd bet it was a '56 or '57.

"I'll take a cab back," he added.

"I appreciate it." I made sure Eliza didn't have any body parts hanging out of the car, then closed the door. I was still nervous, more than nervous, not sure how to broach the subject. "Look, I'd really much rather Nick doesn't find out about this."

Austin raised his eyebrows.

"He's still my boss and we've probably broken half a

dozen liquor licensing regulations, state and local."

Austin shook his head. "This doesn't compare with some of the dumb shit Nick has done but you don't need to worry. I won't tell him."

Still, Nick would care when the dumb shit was done by someone else. They always did.

"Thanks." I grimaced. "Sorry about your shirt. I'll buy you another one."

"No need."

Already unbuttoning the shirt as he walked away, he ripped the thing off, tossed it in a trashcan, and turned to me. He had a few retro tattoos on his arms, a pin-up girl playing upright bass, red and black swallows, a heart, and dagger. No surprises there. No, his chest was the big surprise. Taut skin was stretched across the planes of his chest and not a tattoo in sight to mar the vision of a lean torso and abdominal muscles that rippled as he strode toward me.

I swallowed. I could see exactly why Eliza was so happy to be snuggled against that chest. I melted a little.

Then pulled myself together. My sister had thrown up on him, ruined an expensive shirt, and I was thinking about the planes of his chest. Oh, yes, that was exactly what I was thinking of.

"You'll have to, um, get in the back," I said.

"No problem."

Turned out there was a bit of a problem as he folded himself into the rear of the Micra, only just managed to squeeze in, and we headed off. I opened the windows as I drove.

We didn't say much in the car. Eliza moaned from time to time. She was alive, which was just as well because she'd have to be breathing so I could kill her tomorrow.

I pulled up in the driveway and took a deep breath because my night wasn't over yet. I still had to put Eliza safely in bed. I'd let her sleep it off tomorrow. No point punishing her further by making her go to school in the state she'd be in.

Austin got out and pulled my door open.

"Oh, thank you." I jumped out and raced around to the passenger side to open the door in the hope it'd make his life a little easier.

He leaned over, undid the seat belt, slid one hand under Eliza's thighs. I saw what I hadn't been able to see before, an eagle in full flight on his back, wingtips extending from shoulder to shoulder, talons grasping for prey. I didn't even know an eagle could look retro. Didn't know a tattoo could make me swoon, or maybe it was his muscular back that was doing that to me.

How could I even be swooning at a time like this? I had to get my act together.

"Have you got her?"

By the time I asked, he was already standing. So tall. So strong.

I tried not to stare. "This way."

Racing down the front path, I opened the front door for him. Eliza moaned as soon as I switched the lights on. I hoped Austin wouldn't notice the state of the house. I kept everything clean and made sure Eliza did her share of the housework too, but the place needed work, new floor coverings, new basins in the bathroom, new cupboards in the kitchen, all things that cost money. Somehow it didn't seem so shabby when it was just the two of us at home.

"This way."

I pulled back the covers on Eliza's bed and Austin placed her gently on the sheets while she mumbled words of thanks. Maybe a glimmer of the manners I'd tried to teach her were showing through. Then again, who was I kidding?

"I'll get a glass of water for her," he said. "From the kitchen."

"It's at the end of the hall."

I took off Eliza's shoes and skirt, then pulled the covers over her, brushed the hair from her face, and pressed a kiss to her temple.

Funny how she could look so angelic after everything that had happened tonight. She was only a kid and she'd been through a lot too, lost her mother, lost her father years before that, then Grandma. I wasn't the only one who'd done it hard.

Austin set a glass on the nightstand. "You love her a lot, don't you?"

I nodded, my eyes filling with tears. I didn't even know why. Perhaps it was thinking of the love our mother hadn't given us and the way Gran had helped us more than she could ever know.

So often I felt like I was walking a tightrope. I could bring in a living and manage Eliza and everything else, but then all it took was one little thing to knock me right over. Like tonight.

Austin placed his fingers under my chin, tipped my face up so my eyes met his. All he did was look but it sent my nerve endings tingling. He was so close, looming large in front of me, and it would've been so easy to let someone else take care of me for a change, even someone I barely knew.

"Sorry, I'll call a cab now." He pulled a phone from the pocket of his jeans and stepped out into the hallway.

The moment was gone, which was probably just as well. I stared at my sleeping sister, warmth washing over me before I turned off the light.

I left Eliza's door ajar in case something happened during the night, then bumped into Austin as he got off the phone. It was a tight fit in the hallway. Not hard to bump into him. And not so bad brushing against his muscular arm.

"Cab's on its way," he said.

I lowered my gaze to his bare chest. "You'll need a shirt."

"Sorry?"

"I'll find you a shirt."

He nodded. "Oh, sure."

My bedroom was next to Eliza's so I switched on the light and rummaged through the bottom of one of my drawers until I found what I was after, an oversized burgundy T-shirt from the days of boyfriends past. I'd never had a lot of luck in the boyfriends department. Should have known they were trouble right from the start.

Austin was standing in the doorway, didn't come in. A gentleman.

I shoved the tee shirt into his hands. "Try this."

He pulled it over his head. It didn't look so oversized on him. In fact, he looked positively eye watering even in an old tee shirt.

I swallowed. "I'll walk you to the door."

"Thanks." He turned as we stepped out of the door. "You should get to bed. I'll be fine on the porch."

"I think the least I can do is wait with you until the cab

comes."

At that moment, a car came crawling up the street, the fluorescent sign on its roof unmistakable. A pang shot through me, almost like regret.

"Goodnight, Tara."

"Thanks for everything."

That didn't even begin to sum up the way I felt, my gratitude, my relief at having someone help me through the night.

Closing the door behind me, I made sure it was locked, then pressed my back against it and let out a long sigh.

I looked around. Alone again. Just me and the pang in my chest.

CHAPTER THREE

Austin

"Take a seat, Dad," I said. "I'll get the drinks."

I didn't particularly want a beer but knew my dad would want one. I did, however, want an excuse to go to the bar.

He looked around The Swamp. "This is quite a crowd."

"There's a reason Thursday and Friday lunches are so big here. At least that's what I've heard. Only one way to find out."

Which was true. It was one of the things Nick told me after he bought the bar, probably the only business item he could remember—that Thursday and Friday lunches had a good reputation and brought in more people than anything else.

A bunch of office workers had walked in ahead of us, taking one of the few remaining tables. There was also a group of young women celebrating a birthday and a table of guys in work boots who might've been plumbers or electricians. Talk about a mixed crowd.

Tara stood behind the bar, pouring drinks for an old

couple perched on bar stools, talking animatedly to them, her personality shining through. If she was tired after last night, she wasn't showing it.

She did a double-take when she saw me. And smiled. That was one hell of a smile. Took my breath away. She kept chatting, then made eye contact when I reached the bar.

"You're a fan of The Rev?" she asked.

"Sorry?"

She pointed to my T-shirt. I'd almost forgotten putting on my Reverend Horton Heat shirt this morning. I loved the band. The retro graphics too.

"Yep, a big fan," I said. "So how did your little sister shape up after last night?"

Tara frowned. "If it makes you feel any better, she looked and felt like absolute crap this morning." She held a hand out. "Which she should, especially after what she put you through."

"Well, I'm sure glad that's over. Does she remember much about it?"

"She remembers the bit where she threw up on you."

"Yeah, that's often the way."

"And she told me…" Tara's eyes widened for a moment. "Um, can I get you anything?"

That caught my interest. "What did she tell you?"

Tara sighed. "You might not want to hear it."

"Try me."

"Eliza knew she was going to be sick last night." She hesitated, raising her eyebrows. "But she didn't want to interrupt you while you were talking so, well, you know what happened."

I groaned. "Maybe I shouldn't have asked. Or maybe I

should laugh. It's over with, after all."

"I hope you can laugh because I'm still mortified. I've told Eliza she'd better behave herself or I'll post photos on social media."

"But you didn't take pictures."

Tara smiled. "She doesn't know that, though." She shrugged. "Besides, it's what her friends would do."

A little extra punishment couldn't hurt and might even help when it came to teaching her a lesson. It made me smile too.

"What would you like to drink?" Tara asked.

"The Frankston IPA was pretty good. Two of those, thanks."

"I'll bring them over."

But I didn't want good service. I wanted to spend more time talking to her.

"Look, I was a bit slow last night. Took me a while to get your name, and I don't want to make the same mistake again." I left a meaningful pause, gave her my best smile, hoped I looked suave. "I can't leave without getting your number first."

She poured the first beer, looked at me. "My number?"

"So I can call you. Kind of old fashioned, I know."

She put the first glass down, picked up another, her eyes lowered. "Maybe I'm old fashioned too. I'll bring your drinks over."

That sounded like a 'no', which was not what I was expecting. Something about the look on her face told me there was no point arguing.

"Thanks." Disappointment washing over me, I turned away. Not that I was giving up. Just taking a break.

I joined my dad at a table in the corner. He was still

looking around, checking the place out. Not a lot got past him. He watched as another group of people wandered in.

"I'm surprised," he said. "This place seems to be doing good business."

"For now. It's not so busy the rest of the time."

"So how was the party last night?"

I didn't want to go into details. "It was packed. Every man and his dog was here."

Dad smiled. "Not me, I didn't get an invite. I must be too old."

I spread my arms. "Hey, last night *I* was bordering on being too old."

Tara brought our drinks over, slid them onto the table on a couple of coasters, and handed us each a menu.

"Tara, this is my father, David," I said.

"Your dad? No kidding?" She raised her eyebrows in mock surprise then shook Dad's hand. "That's quite a family resemblance."

We looked alike. Everyone told me that, even if sometimes it was hard for me to see. We were both architects too. I'd followed in my father's footsteps at first, then followed my dream of playing in a band and now I was chasing something else. Always chasing something.

Despite this, Dad and I were quite different. I wasn't judgmental like him or nearly as conservative. At least I hoped I wasn't.

He nodded toward me. "Wish I still had that head of hair."

"On the contrary." Tara placed a hand on her hip. "Your silver hair is so dashing."

Dad couldn't stop smiling as he had a sip of beer. "Nice and dry, just how I like it."

"Like your sense of humor."

"But I haven't made a joke yet."

"Bet I'm right, though."

He smiled, nodded. I picked up a menu to check if Tara might have written her number on it, but the damn thing was laminated and she hadn't deposited any other mysterious bits of paper on the table.

"I'll come back after you've worked out what you're having," she said.

"No need." I knew our order because Dad had told me what he wanted before we got here. "A cheeseburger for me and the steak for my father please."

Tara picked up our menus. "With fries?"

"Of course."

"No point living without fries."

She turned away all too quickly. Another opportunity lost. I drummed my fingers on the table.

"What's up?" Dad asked.

I didn't answer. "So what do you think of the place?"

He scoffed. "Is that a serious question?"

"It's a dump, and dumps need to be renovated."

Thoughtful now. "So you think Nick will need an architect?"

"He's going to need more than an architect. As soon as he stops partying and starts thinking about this seriously, he'll work it out."

"And you can give him a little push in the right direction."

I nodded. "Absolutely."

"What does he want to turn the place into?"

"We're not talking redevelopment. Far as I know, Nick wants to update and renovate. God knows, the place needs it. I gather this'll still be a bar, still have bands, still keep doing what it's doing, only better."

I gave him a rundown of the history of the place. Dad had always been into the music of the '50s even though that was before his time—that was probably where I got my interest in rockabilly—but he wasn't so much into live gigs, which is why he'd never been here before.

My father did, however, understand architecture. He was never going to be Frank Lloyd Wright designing the Guggenheim or William Van Alen designing The Chrysler Building, my personal favorite, but Dad was good at what he did and had made a name for himself in Frankston.

Our meals arrived—delivered by someone else—and we ate and talked.

"Excellent," Dad said. "Maybe I should give Nick a call."

"Not just yet. Leave it with me."

He gave me a dour expression. "I didn't get ahead by not following up on leads."

"Nick needs a little more time. I'm right here and he's not going anywhere in a hurry."

The severe look continued. "Clients don't grow on trees, you know. You can't just leave these things or someone else will get in first."

I didn't want to get into it right now. I needed time to talk to Nick. And the other guys. It was only right that they heard the news from me first. Didn't matter that my father could keep a secret. That wasn't what this was about.

I held a hand out. "Just this once, Dad."

He nodded. Kept up the disgruntled look.

After a long silence, he pushed away his plate. "When you invited me here, I thought you might have some big announcement."

I stiffened. It was big all right, so big it had been weighing me down.

"You ever think about getting back into architecture?" he asked.

"Hmm, might be a bit too soon."

A question my father asked me every time I came back home, a question I used to laugh off because I was living the dream, making lots of money, playing in a rock band, living the life, constant partying, girls chasing me. A bottomless supply.

Until Reno, where everything changed. It'd been three in the morning and I'd only just managed to fall asleep after our concert when there was a knocking at my door. I'd got up to find a young woman had dropped to her knees, offering to blow me right there in the doorway. It wasn't so much the offer that'd shaken me up as how quickly she'd managed to pull my shorts down. Right off, in fact, so I'd stood there with my dick hanging out. Until I'd somehow managed to get rid of her.

It had freaked me out big time. Gave me an inkling of just how outrageous fans could be. It might've been some other guy's dream but it made me feel disturbed and dirty.

Reno, the town where Johnny Cash killed a man to watch him die. Part of me had died right there too.

"You were always building stuff as a kid." Dad was smiling now. "It all started with Duplo. And drawing. You were always drawing. And that coffee table you made in high school is a wonderful piece of design."

I smiled too, letting my father reminisce like he did every time I was back. It was better than thinking about Reno.

Despite the fact he wasn't normally sentimental, he'd hung onto many of my 'pieces' as he called them. Meanwhile, I'd given Mom some of my framed paintings because I knew she'd love them.

We'd started off as a happy family and then after my parents divorced, I'd lived with Dad, and Julia had lived with Mom. Not exactly ideal but at least my parents had been civil to each other, even if I'm not sure how happy Dad was when Mom remarried and moved away last year.

"It's a shame not to use skills like yours," Dad said. "You're good with your hands, good at designing, good at lots of things."

I leaned back in my chair. "Wow, you sound like a proud father."

"Nothing wrong with that. Besides, it's true."

"I'm back for a while. Let's just wait and see how things pan out."

"Certainly, son." He pushed his chair back. "I'll just go and wash my hands, then I've got to get back to work."

"Sure."

I turned to look for Tara, only to find she was heading my way. I liked watching the swing of her hips, the gentle jiggle of her boobs under her T-shirt, the smile on her lips. There were a lot of things I liked and something about the way she made me feel that set me on edge. In the best way possible.

"I was just on a break," she said. "And I checked my phone. Eliza asked me to tell you again how sorry she is. She's genuinely ashamed about last night, embarrassed that you're here, and mortified you might tell anyone what happened."

"I won't." I shook my head. "I don't particularly want

to go there again."

"I'll tell her that... soon. In the meantime, I'll let her wallow a little."

My first ever drinking episode came to mind, followed by the hangover from hell. "Don't be too hard on her."

"Well, she's got to learn about consequences. I can't just let her get away with this stuff."

"You sound like a parent."

She rolled her eyes. "Sometimes I feel like one too."

"Why?"

Her face clouded over. "Eliza's only got me. Our mom died a couple of years ago."

"I'm sorry. I didn't realize. So you look after Eliza now?"

"Yep."

"Then she's lucky to have you."

"I'm lucky too. Eliza's a dream compared to me as a teenager. She was terrible last night, I know, but she's not normally like that. She studies hard and gets excellent grades, that's one thing I don't have to worry about." Tara had a hint of the proud parent look my father had been sporting earlier on. "I don't even know where she gets it from."

"Not from you?"

She shrugged, a simple act that made her look alluring. "I was never one for studying. Don't suppose you were either. You probably spent all your time practicing the bass and playing with the band."

"Actually..."

"Actually what?"

"I'm an architect. It's what I did before the band took off."

Her mouth formed a perfect O. "Really?"

But the trepidation in her eyes told me this wasn't a good 'really'.

At that moment Dad came through the door at the far end of the room.

I stood, turned to Tara. "So, ah, about your number?"

"Old fashioned, remember." She piled up the plates from the table, left before Dad got back.

I sighed, then it hit me. She'd left the glasses on the table, the coasters too, probably coming back for them later. I shifted the glass, picked up the coaster, and looked on the underside. Sure enough, she'd written her phone number on the bottom. Success at last.

"Are you ready?" Dad asked.

I pocketed the coaster. "I am now."

When we reached the door, I turned to see Tara at the far end of the room, leaning against the bar, smiling. She winked at me but I had the feeling she was holding something back.

Dad put his arm around me, probably still doing the proud father thing. "It's good to have you back in town, son."

"Good for me too."

He was probably going to be happy when he found out what was going on. Meanwhile, I was stressed as all hell about it even though I knew it was the right decision. It was a big change, a huge lifestyle shift, a significant drop in income too, not that I cared about money that much.

I cared about my friends, though. A lot.

And they weren't going to be happy when I told them I was leaving The Merchants.

CHAPTER FOUR

Tara

Why did life have to be so complicated? Surely things weren't this difficult for other people.

Austin had been texting and calling, not so much that he was badgering but enough so I knew he was interested. It was nice of him. More than nice. Hell, 'nice' didn't even begin to cover it, but I had so much to think about at the moment.

Because I kept wondering if I'd been doing something wrong with Eliza. I was doing my best, though I'd probably been spending too much time at work and not enough with her. Maybe she needed me to keep a closer eye on her.

One thing was for sure. I wasn't going to be like our mother. I was going to be there for my little sister.

A book tucked under my arm, phone in hand, I headed to the kitchen for a glass of water before stepping outside. Eliza stood behind the sink, gazing out of the window. Unusual for her because even if she was flaked out on the sofa, she'd be on her phone and watching TV at the same time.

"Are you okay?" I asked.

"Huh, yeah, fine."

"You're still not yourself, are you?"

"My head's a bit fuzzy, that's all."

"Must be a very nasty hangover if it's still lingering."

She straightened. "No way. That's the most ridiculous thing I've heard. There's no such thing as a three-day hangover."

I'd had one of those myself many years ago but wasn't about to tell her that. God knows, I didn't want her doing some of the stupid things I'd done. When I was at school, I'd cut class until there was no more class left to cut. I'd never gone anywhere near drugs but I used to get drunk all the time. I'd get into cars with speeding drivers, with guys I barely knew, all of which had seemed like a good idea at the time. I'd run away from home too, not that there was much of a home to run away from. The list went on.

I couldn't be too hard on Eliza when she was an angel compared to me during my teenage years.

I poured a glass of water but the faucet kept dripping. I tightened the lever and stared. Two seconds later, it dripped again.

"Are you going to change the washer?" Eliza asked.

I'd already done that. Twice. The thing was so ancient it was beyond fixing.

"I might have to bite the bullet and buy a new faucet," I said. "It'll mean getting a plumber in."

"It'd be nice to have one of those mixer ones."

"Yeah, it would."

In another life, maybe. I looked down at the linoleum tiles that were coming up at the corners, not that the floor was crumbling beneath our feet, only the floor coverings so maybe it wasn't so bad. But sometimes it dragged me down, the run-down state of this place, this feeling that we'd never be able to get ahead, that I was barely able to provide enough for us to get by.

"Just as well Grandma had her shit together." The words slipped out.

"What?"

I only spoke of our grandmother with the utmost respect. This was probably the first time I'd used the word 'shit' in the same sentence as her name.

"It's true," I said. "We owe a lot to her."

This was Grandma's house. She'd always lived in Frankston whereas we'd moved around a lot, shifting to a different town every couple of years—for a fresh start supposedly, but usually because Mom was bored and once because she was running away from a drug dealer.

Then she'd overdosed a few years ago. An accident. It hadn't killed her. That time. I'd worked out things were bad and quickly relocated to Frankston where she and Eliza were living at the time.

The second overdose did kill her. I'll never forget the phone call from Eliza, who'd found Mom's body. And the guilt. Because I should've seen it coming and should have been able to protect my sister.

After that, the two of us moved in with Grandma, who'd insisted on it and had loved us to bits. Not long afterward, Grandma died. Natural causes. A stroke. That's what they said, because doctors didn't understand people could die from a broken heart.

She left us the house and we were damned lucky to have it. I'd rather have Grandma with us but that wasn't my choice to make. I swallowed the lump in my throat because I had more than just respect for Grandma. 'Love' was a whole different ball game.

"Thanks," Eliza said.

"For what?"

"For not drinking and smoking and doing drugs."

She threw her arms around me. Depositing my book and phone on the countertop, I hugged her right back, held her tight because you had to hold the people you loved close. Warmth flooded through me. This was why I lived, what made it all worthwhile, my reason for being.

Such a slender thing, Eliza felt fragile in my grasp and it only made me want to take care of her even more. Tears sprang to my eyes, tears I held back because I had to be strong.

"Let's go out to the patio," I said. "You need a break from studying."

"I guess I could chill for a bit."

We headed outside. Eliza was probably the only teenager who needed to be reminded to take a break when she was studying. Sometimes it was as if she was two people—the diligent student and the silly girl who hung out with Michaela.

I dropped down onto one of the plastic chairs that looked out onto the garden, put my book on the table.

"How's your English essay going?" I asked.

Eliza sat on the chair next to me, staring straight ahead at the garden. "Why did Mom choose drugs over us?"

Whoa, where had that come from? What else was going on in her mind? I took a deep breath because if my sister was ready to talk, then I had to be too.

"She was an addict, honey. She made a bad choice early on, took drugs, kept taking them, and then she was stuck. She couldn't give it up."

"She gave it up for a few years."

"Yeah, she did."

And I'd made the mistake of thinking it was okay for me to leave them and move away to the big smoke. I'd lived in New York for a while, then moved upstate. Seemed like a good idea at the time.

"So why didn't Mom stay clean?"

Eliza was matter-of-fact, no tears in her eyes, and maybe she was hardened to this too. That might've been the saddest thing of all, that she'd had part of her childhood taken away.

"I don't have a good answer for you, honey. She should've stayed off the drugs, should've been a proper mother to you, but she didn't do any of those things. Addiction is a terrible thing."

"It was terrible for me too. For us."

I reached for my sister's hand. It broke my heart that Eliza had been through so much, that she'd had hope only to have it snatched away from her, that I hadn't been there for her. It wasn't surprising that sometimes she did something stupid like the other night.

And it astounded me that she never used any of this as an excuse to slack off at school. My little sister was an amazing young woman. No wonder I was so damn proud of her.

"Mom loved you, honey," I said. "You've got to believe that."

"But she loved the drugs more."

Desperation dripped from her voice, sank deep into my bones because I felt it too, the defeat and the failure, the feeling that I wasn't good enough, of helplessness too.

At least Eliza could lean on me. It was something.

My phone pinged so I glanced down and saw a message from Austin. My heart skipped a beat but I turned away and pretended I didn't care.

"Who was that?" Eliza asked.

"Austin."

"Oh, so you're on first name terms with him?"

I laughed it off. "I'm not going to call him Mr. Murphy."

"What does *Austin* want?" She smiled, her tone teasing.

"That doesn't really matter, not when we were have a deep discussion."

"I'm done talking. About that, anyway." She glanced down at my phone. "Sooo?"

I might as well tell her. "He's asking if I want him to come around with a tub from Peppe's Gelato."

Her eyes widened. "Yes, yes, yes, of course we do!"

"I'm not so sure."

It wasn't that I didn't want to see him. I did. But I was in the middle of something with Eliza.

Who whacked me on the shoulder. "Well, *I'm* sure. He has to come over, he has to!"

"Why?"

"I got him a shirt."

"Really? That's nice of you but how did you afford it?"

She pointed to my phone. "Text first. Talk later."

"Okay." I messaged Austin and he responded immediately, saying he was on his way before I'd even put the phone down. It made me smile.

"Just as well." Eliza rolled her eyes. "I can't possibly get back to my English essay until I've had ice cream."

I raised my eyebrows. "The shirt?"

"Oh, I went shopping after school yesterday, saw it in the window of a recycling store and knew it was the right one. Second-hand so I could afford it but really good. And I know he'll like it because it's the same sort of old retro stuff that you like."

Perhaps Eliza had got a lot off her chest because she seemed back to her old self. Later the doorbell rang so I went to get the door while she raced to her room to get the shirt.

I opened the front door. Different day, different cool T-shirt, same broad chest. The man was smokin'. Also, nothing said 'hello' like ice cream, and Peppe's was the best in town.

Then I saw it. The 1956 Thunderbird parked on the street, whitewall tires, an opera window in the hard top, pearlescent paint that shone pale pink and green in the sun. The only car that could send a pang straight through my heart.

Eliza raced up from behind. "Cool car. Tara loves those things."

I stood and admired and maybe even swooned. "What I wouldn't give to have a car like that, my dream car."

"Hey." Austin grinned. "Aren't I a dream guy?"

He had no idea how far out of my reach a vintage Thunderbird was, but maybe he was right because he was a dream too.

Eliza grabbed Austin's arm. "Quick, before the ice cream melts."

"Come through." I managed to pull myself together. "I'll get bowls and spoons."

He stepped inside. "So you're not one of these girls

who eats straight from the tub?"

"Actually, I'm a girl who shares, and we've gotta share with Eliza. Hope that's okay." I pointed ahead while I made a quick detour to the kitchen. "Straight ahead out onto the patio."

When I got outside, Eliza was holding a gift bag out to Austin. "This is for you."

He placed a hand on his chest. "For me?"

"To say sorry for the other night because I am really, really sorry. And embarrassed. And if it's okay I'd rather we didn't talk about it because we've done a lot of talking. So can you please just open the bag."

He took the bag and pulled out the shirt—blue with white piping and a palm tree motif embroidered on the yokes above the pockets. It was kind of weird and exactly right.

"Do you like it?" Eliza looked up at him, her voice small.

Austin didn't say anything right away, just stared. Then, "I'm touched."

"But do you like it?"

"It's perfect." Sliding one arm around her, he gave her shoulder a quick squeeze. "You nailed it."

"So that means I'm forgiven?"

"Yes." He looked at her through hooded brows. "Just don't do it again."

"I won't."

Sometimes she sounded like a little girl again. It made my heart swell.

I interrupted them. "The ice cream is about to melt, remember?"

I scooped up two generous servings plus a small one

for Austin because he said he didn't have much of a sweet tooth, put the remaining ice cream in the freezer, and rushed back.

"You've got a lot of tattoos," Eliza said between mouthfuls while I sat down.

Austin looked down at his arms. "A few."

"I saw your back the other night."

"Really?"

"I opened my eyes for a bit. You were blurry but I could still tell that thing was big." She turned to me. "Do you have any tattoos?"

"No." None I was going to own up to. Talk about taking me by surprise.

Eliza picked up my phone and passed it to me. "Can you take a photo?" She sidled closer to Austin who put his arm around her. "It'll make the other girls so jealous." As soon as the photo was taken, she changed the subject again. "You must be excited about playing The Flats."

"Um, yeah," he said.

"Well, everyone knows you're back in town for The Flats Festival and for your new record. When will that be out? I mean, how long does it take to record an album?"

"How long is a piece of string?" He held a hand out. "You're going a bit fast for me."

"For me too," I said. "Don't you have homework to do?"

"I can take a hint, you know." Eliza picked up her empty bowl, hesitated, then pressed a quick kiss to Austin's cheek. "Glad you like the shirt."

She could be such a sweetie. Austin was grinning as she left.

"It's been a while since I've been around a teenage

girl," he said.

"Wish I could say the same." I laughed. "Would you like some coffee?"

"Sure."

He followed me to the kitchen, which wasn't part of the plan. Embarrassment washed over me—at the faucet that dripped, at the state of the floor coverings, at the paint peeling from the window frames because I hadn't gotten to them yet.

"I changed the washer." I poured water into the pod coffee machine while I talked. "Didn't help."

"Hmm."

I waited for the machine to do its magic. "I make good coffee, though. Coffee is important."

"Sure is."

I didn't add the rest. *And I can afford it.*

We stayed in the kitchen, sipping our coffee, both of us leaning against the countertops, and eventually, the dripping stopped.

"I see what you meant about your sister." He held my gaze. "She sounds like a good kid. It also seems good looks run in your family."

I smiled. "I could say the same about yours."

"I'm nothing like my father, though."

"Something else we have in common because I'm nothing like my mother." Not a story I'd get into right now.

"What about your dad? Is he around?"

"He left when I was eight."

Never to be seen again. He'd left despite the fact Eliza had been a baby, or maybe because of it. Which was why I tried not to think of him. He wasn't worth it.

Austin raised his eyebrows. "He didn't keep in touch?"

"No. I don't have a clue where he is and don't want to know."

"He's an idiot, then. He's missed out on watching his two wonderful daughters grow up. Well, one of them still has a bit of growing to do, but you get the idea."

Warmth washed over me. "Such a nice thing for you to say."

"Are you doing anything tonight?"

"Working." I shrugged. "A gal's got to work."

"What about tomorrow?"

"My day off."

"Great, I'll pick you at around five."

Something sizzled deep in my belly. I liked the sound of this.

"But you didn't even ask me if I wanted to go out?"

"Nope. The nice guy approach wasn't working so well for me."

A hand on my chest, I threw my head back and feigned shock. "So presumptuous of you."

He put his coffee down, cupped my chin in his hands, and pressed his lips against mine. The warmth from my stomach spread through to my limbs, made me relaxed and tense at the same time.

No hesitation, I liked that. Soft lips. I liked that too.

He stepped away, smiled, looked good enough to eat. "See you tomorrow. I'll see myself out."

"Hey," I said. "I didn't know you were the love 'em and leave 'em type."

Grinning now. "Next time you won't be able to get rid of me."

And he left.

I wasn't sure I wanted to. Get rid of him, that was. Maybe it wouldn't be so bad having a man around the house after all.

CHAPTER FIVE

Austin

It had been a long time since I'd been on a proper date, not since before we'd left town and hit the road for those first grueling tours after I first joined the band four years ago.

They were the best of times and the worst of times. Who'd said that? Was it Dickens? There had been so many good things going on in my life at the time. I knew exactly how good the band was back then, better than good. Shit hot. We were pumped up and excited. Our sound had been so raw and energetic then. Less so now.

And everything had been new, even for me, the 'old guy' of the band. It'd been hard quitting my job because I'd wanted to be an architect since I was a kid, but that probably just showed how much I loved my music too. And the opportunity of a lifetime.

Looking back, I probably hadn't been on a proper date since I first started seeing Philippa all those years ago. So strange to be dating again at thirty. With The Merchants, there'd been girls, plenty of girls. It hadn't reached the sophistication levels of actual dating, though. Pathetic, really.

I glanced around the wine bar restaurant, high ceilings, dark walls, light pooling over the tables, the rest of the room dark. A friend had recommended the place to me. I'd have to buy him a beer because this place had sophistication and romance written all over it.

I looked back at Tara. I'd much rather be looking at her. She took my breath away.

"Have you been here before?" I asked.

"No, I work most nights. Don't go out that much."

And maybe she couldn't afford it. I'd worked that much out.

"Frankston has changed a lot over the years," I said. "It wasn't like this when I was a kid or even five years ago. Now there are laneways lined with cafes, little bars that have popped up all over the place, and it's even more 'happening' than before."

"I don't know what the place was like five years ago," she said. "My gran had always lived here and we used to visit her, but it's different when you're visiting. We just hung at her place mostly or went to her favorite diner. Didn't venture too much further."

"Everyone should have a favorite diner. Life's not all about five-star restaurants. If you can't appreciate a good burger or a piece of homemade pie, you're missing out."

She smiled. "Nice to hear you say that."

It wasn't all about the money for her. So different from Philippa who hadn't had time for the musician in me, my creative side, not if I wasn't making an income. As soon as I'd started talking about quitting my day job, she dumped me because she wasn't going to support me in any way, shape, or form.

Then came back when she realized I wasn't a struggling musician anymore. Or tried to come back. By then, The Merchants of Menace were making waves in the industry, getting big deals thanks to our manager, and making serious money.

So often the music business brought out the worst in people. I could never have guessed my girlfriend would be one of those people.

Still, I should've known it wouldn't last. Nothing ever did. I shouldn't even be thinking about 'her' when I had someone so much better right in front of me.

"So what's the secret to The Swamp's busy lunches?" I asked.

"Only two days are busy, Thursdays and Fridays. Kitchen's closed on the other days, which is complete madness because we could make a killing on the weekends."

"So why don't you open?"

A dull expression on her face. "I'm not the manager."

"Did you tell the previous owner?"

"He wasn't interested. I think he'd been looking to offload the place for a while."

"Have you talked to Nick?"

She shook her head. "He's only just got back to town. I'll talk to him soon, though. It's frustrating when I can see some easy fixes that'd bring in more business. The place could be doing so much better with stronger management."

"What about you?"

"What *about* me?"

"Is that what you'd like to do? Go into management."

She couldn't keep the smile from her face, such a

pretty face. "It's what I've always wanted to do, manage a bar, and I could do such a good job if I had the chance. I don't want to sound full of myself but I've got the experience."

"And the nous?"

"Yep. It takes a lot of skills to be a good manager. It's not just one thing. It's lots of things. You need to be on the ball all the time, keep your eye on the market, know what else is happening. You can't let things slip. You need to be organized, see what's working and what's not, and be able to give clear directions to the staff."

I smiled. Couldn't help it. "You don't seem to have a problem telling people what to do."

"Sorry?"

"Like the other night, when Nick started trashing the band room. You gave him what for."

A sheepish look on her face. "I had to. I've seen what can happen. The last two bars I worked at went out of business."

"So that's why you took the job at The Swamp?"

"At such a dump, yeah." She nodded. "And now maybe, I don't know, maybe I'd have a chance at being bar manager. I could help bring the place back to life and, for me, it'd be more responsibility, more money too."

And make a big difference to her, no doubt. Something tugged at my heart, not because of the money side of things but because of everything. On the outside Tara was hardened, a hard worker too, wouldn't take shit from anyone.

I'd seen glimpses of a different person on the inside, softer, caring, a young woman who'd do anything for her sister. That was one hell of a responsibility and I couldn't see even a glimmer of resentment or any sign that this was a burden. All of that for someone she loved.

"I can talk to the boss." I smiled. "I know him well."

How could I have come out with that? I desperately wanted to help her but that would be no help at all. Nick wouldn't be doing me any favors, not after I told the guys I was leaving the band.

It sent a shudder up my spine. I dreaded letting them down, but I couldn't keep being part of something that simply wasn't 'me'. And I couldn't explain any of this to Tara until I'd talked to the guys first. They deserved at least that much.

She shook her head. "Not while Nick's drunk and not until I've had a chance to make a better impression."

Relief washed over me. "You made an impression, all right."

"Yeah, that's part of the problem."

Our meals arrived and we kept talking. She wasn't one of those people who spilled their guts all at once and that was okay because I wasn't one of those people who gave up, not when I wanted something. Or someone, in this case.

"What did you think of the band?" I asked.

Before dinner, we'd been to see a local band, The Chevelles, at a dive bar, also local. We'd found we had mutual friends, always a good thing. Frankston was that kind of town when you were into a small scene like rockabilly.

"They were fun," she said. "They played all my favorite songs, the Elvis classics, a bit of Carl Perkins."

"All the standards."

"Yeah, I like to hear new stuff too sometimes, their

own songs, some originals."

"Good bass player. There's nothing like an upright bass to capture that sound."

I missed my upright. Might be getting back to it soon. I was desperate to get back to my roots and do my own thing. It was liberating. And also slightly scary.

The upright had never suited the modern grungy sound of The Merchants, had never been right, just like my songs weren't quite right. So often I felt like the George Harrison of the band. My songs had to be absolute killers before the guys would even think about putting one of them on the record, a token effort on their part. I'd nailed it with *Linger in the Lounge* and the song was a hit but that didn't change things, not in the long run.

I couldn't be 'me' in that band. Only with rockabilly could I could truly let it rip and get down and dirty.

A waiter cleared our plates. I knew the drill. Soon he'd be back to ask if we wanted coffee or dessert. Tara said thank you, smiled at him, her eyes crinkling at the corners. She was wearing a high-necked number that kept her covered but showed off her pretty shoulders and collar bones. Her skin was so pale, so soft, so close. I wanted dessert, all right, but not the kind they served here.

She leaned forward. "Have you always lived in Frankston?"

"Yeah, um, no."

Tara frowned, a little crease forming in her otherwise perfect brow and no wonder when I'd given a dumb answer.

I had to get my head together. "We moved here from North Carolina over twenty years ago. Lost everything in a hurricane, then decided to start over somewhere else."

"Everything?"

"Mom saved the photo albums and a few other things. It was hard. I remember my sister crying, Mom too, while Dad and I were in shock. I remember my amazement that something as big as a house could be blown to pieces in a matter of hours."

An emotion that had never quite left me. Not a feeling that life is frail, not exactly. More that it didn't matter how hard you worked or what you did, it could all be ripped from under your feet.

"I walked around in a daze for a long time after that, wondering what was going to fall apart next. Turned out it was my parents' marriage."

"Oh. I didn't know. You seem so … steady that I thought you must've had a stable upbringing."

"Despite those things, it was steady. It left me grounded."

"Yep, very grounded for a rock star."

Not for long. The words I couldn't come out with. "I am but a humble bass player."

"Yep, humble."

Glancing across, Tara saw the waiter heading our way, then leaned forward. "Let's have coffee at your place."

"Sure."

I asked the waiter for the check and held a hand out to Tara so she didn't offer to pay. It was the kind of thing she might feel she had to do and, as much as I appreciated the thought, that was the last thing I wanted.

Taking her hand, I led her through the restaurant. It was freezing outside at night, typical Nevada, so I put my arm around her as we walked.

She'd left her car in a small parking lot around the

corner. I'd wanted to drive but Tara had given me this big story about she couldn't bear to sit in the T-Bird when it could never be hers. I loved that car. It was like a part of me. But Tara had been so insistent that I'd gone along with it.

Keys in her hand, she unlocked the Micra as we walked. Desire coursed through me, sudden and hard. I wasn't going to wait. I'd waited long enough.

I grabbed her arm and spun her around. She was pressed against her car, her lips parted, skin so pale. Her hair was dark in the dim light, so dark you couldn't see the purple streak, but those blue eyes were sparkling. At me.

My lips were parted too as I leaned closer and pressed my mouth against hers, gently at first, partway between teasing and testing. She looked at me through those lush lashes, her eyes dewy now.

Screw being gentle. I wrapped my arms around her waist, pressed myself against her, covered her mouth with mine, and kissed her the way I wanted to, kissed her like I meant it. Because I did. Her tongue rolled against mine and I could've sworn it went straight to my dick, drove me crazy.

The jingle of keys as they hit the ground rang through the air. Meanwhile, she dug her hands into the back of my neck, pulled me closer. I cupped her breast with one hand, felt its softness, felt her waiting for me. My hands went lower, pulling up her skirt. Damn that tight skirt. Her hands were unbuttoning my shirt, then on my chest. She was panting, hungry.

Jesus, what was I doing? In a parking lot. I wanted her but not like this.

I groaned. "You wanted to drive. Now drive."

Tara pushed me away, those delicate little hands on my chest. I stepped back, gave her some space. God knows, I needed it too. She bent over to pick up her keys. I should've done that for her, should've been a gentleman, except I couldn't get my eyes off the way that dress cupped her butt. This woman had curves that could kill.

I let out a long sigh. Hoped she was going to speed all the way. She had the keys now so I held the door open for her. Got in the other side.

"Your place," she said.

"Russell Street is the quickest way of getting there."

The next ten minutes were the longest of my life as I tried to make polite conversation when 'polite' was the last thing I wanted to be.

When we finally got to my house, Tara slipped her hand into mine as I walked in, switched on the hall light.

"I don't really want coffee," she said.

Perfect because neither did I.

"Which way is the bedroom?" she asked.

"I'll show you."

Her hand still in mine, I led her into the bedroom and switched on the bedside lamp, bathing the room in a soft glow. For a minute, we held hands, staring into each other's eyes. And somehow I knew that this was 'before' and soon there would be 'after'. I felt it deep inside, because nothing about Tara was ordinary.

Breaking the spell, she snaked her arms around my neck and kissed me hard. I slid my hands onto her waist, kissed her back. Soon, it would all happen soon.

She pushed me onto the bed, then reached behind to slide down the zipper of her dress, the sound of plastic grating on plastic loud in the silence of the room. Her hands still behind her, she unclasped her bra, a black lacy thing. No padding, none needed.

Those breasts were magnificent, mesmerizing. I couldn't get my eyes off them. Had to get my hands on them. I reached, stopped in mid-air, as I watched her slide her panties down her hips and kick them away. Blood pumped through my body, straight to my dick.

God, I was wearing way too many clothes. Tara ripped my shirt apart and tossed it to the floor while I shucked off my jeans, grabbing a condom from the pocket.

The first time was quick, urgent, impatient. I wasn't the only one who needed it there and then. Afterward we went slower, exploring each other's bodies, taking our time. I could've spent hours caressing her breasts, taking her nipples into my mouth, massaging those magnificent handfuls. Then there was the dip of her waist, the curve of her hips. The way she panted short and fast, then that high-pitched moan as she came, the pleasure that sound gave me, the excitement of her hand wrapped around my cock. Then her mouth wrapped around it. I could've died right then.

Afterward, we lay in each other's arms. Naked, of course. I liked her that way. She looked good in clothes, had her own style. Looked even better out of them. It made me wish we could stay this way all the time, just the two of us, *au naturale*, no one to bother us, no worries in the world.

Right now the only thing I had to worry about was getting a drink because I was thirsty as all hell.

I sat up in bed. "Can I bring you a glass of wine? Some cold water?"

She rolled onto her stomach, her head still stuffed in

the pillow. "Water, yes."

Then I saw what I hadn't seen before. A tattoo of the Chrysler Building on her ass. So perfect it made me smile. Not the tallest building, not by a long shot, but one of the most iconic in the world. How could she have known I loved art deco and that this was my favorite building in New York? Man, this woman was made for me.

Leaning over, I pressed a kiss to her butt.

"What are you...?" She rolled onto her side, looked down her body to where my face was hovering. "Oh, I forgot."

I sat up. "You said you didn't have any tattoos."

"Just the one." A guilty look on her face. "I never bothered telling Eliza about it. Didn't want to set a bad example."

"This is bad?"

"I was young, didn't know what I was doing, didn't fully understand how permanent this would be." She threw one hand up. "Sounds silly, I know."

I raised my eyebrows. "It's about as permanent as you can get."

She shrugged. "The tattoos aren't really 'me'. The clothes, the hair, all those things are part of my personality but the tattoo was just a passing phase. Except it's not passing."

I pressed a quick kiss to her cheek. "I'll be back with some water."

She stood up, beat me to it. "I'll come with you."

The only thing better than lying in bed with a naked Tara was walking through the house with her. Her hair tumbled over her shoulders, hips swaying, breasts jiggling. I could turn into a nudist if we kept this up.

I switched on the kitchen light and dug two glasses out of the cupboard while she looked around like a little kid with stars in her eyes. The place probably seemed like a mansion to her. To me, it was just a house. I'd bought the place a few years ago so I had somewhere to stay when I was back in town, but I hadn't designed it. For one thing, I would've made the kitchen smaller because a guy like me didn't need a huge family kitchen.

"This is a bit too glitzy for my taste," I said.

Tara's eyes widened. "No, I love it."

I poured two glasses of water from the dispenser on the fridge, one thing I did like about the kitchen because I'd chosen it myself.

"Ooh, you've got one of those." She drank and put the glass down, then turned and motioned for me to follow her. Back to the bedroom. No arguing from me.

She stood at the edge of the bed, facing me. "I should go."

"You should stay."

I took one nipple into my mouth, taking pleasure in my hands on her breasts, in the moan that escaped her lips.

She dropped back down onto the bed. "We could be quick."

Or we could be slow. Or somewhere in between. We could do whatever we wanted because there was nothing else in the world, just me and Tara, enjoying each other's bodies, savoring every square inch, every moment, every moan.

We weren't quick. We were probably both starting to tire and it was getting late. As we lay together afterward, I couldn't help but think how my first impression of her was so, so right. A firecracker. An explosion. A detonator.

That'd be a good name for a band. The Detonators. Because I wanted to start a new band where I could play my own songs, do my own thing, even if it wasn't as huge as The Merchants. In fact, it'd be better if I kept things small. Just gigs on the weekend. Maybe a regular gig, that'd be nice.

My eyes were closed, my mind drifting off. Such a lovely way to go to sleep. A beautiful woman in my arms. Not just any woman. Tara.

Movement. My arms felt cold, my eyes springing open. Tara was sitting on the edge of the bed, the back of her dress not yet zipped, putting her shoes on.

She wriggled a little. "Can you zip me up please?"

No. Get back in bed. "What are you doing?"

"I have to go."

"No, you don't."

She glared, gave me the sort of look I knew there'd be no arguing with. I moaned, zipped up her dress.

"I'll see myself out." Leaning across, she kissed me on the lips.

"Why are you going? Stay here with me."

She blew me another kiss from the doorway and then she was gone. I lay back on the bed, my hands clasped at the back of my neck.

What was going on with her? Eliza was sixteen, old enough to be home alone for one night. Tara was an adult and I was ... I thought I was someone she cared about. It didn't make sense. It wasn't as though she had to get up early in the morning and even if she did, she had an alarm on her phone.

Then it hit me. That was why she wanted to drive

tonight, why she wanted to come back to my place and not hers.

So she could leave.

CHAPTER SIX

Tara

Back when the two of us were living with Mom in whatever town we'd parked our asses in for a year or two, I used to help Eliza with her homework. She was eight years younger than me so there was a pretty good chance I'd be able to manage her schoolwork. And I'd liked it. It had never been too much trouble for me. I'd always made the time for her.

How things had changed. I'd love to be able to give her a hand but since there was nothing on the school syllabus about how to make the perfect mojito, the chances of that were pretty slim.

She leaned against the kitchen countertop. "This physics stuff is killing me."

"Wish I could help, honey."

"I tried Carson but even he couldn't help and he's probably the smartest kid in the class when it comes to this electricity crap."

I raised my eyebrows. "Electricity crap?"

"It's what they make me study at school."

She'd chosen the subject but I didn't argue the point.

Unfortunately, school had never been my thing. By the time I was fourteen, I was too busy trying to get paid jobs to worry about school—babysitting, cleaning, and other odd jobs, then my first 'real' job at the supermarket. I'd needed the money. Because we didn't have any.

Then it came to me. "Do you want me to see if Austin can help?"

She sighed. "If you think it's worth a try."

I did. Austin wasn't so sure that 'electricity crap' was his specialty but he came over anyway, didn't waste any time. By the time he arrived, Eliza had finished moping and had set herself up at the dining table so they wouldn't be cramped in her room.

I greeted Austin at the door. Couldn't stop myself from smiling because he looked good enough to eat. Ushering him inside, I forced myself to keep the conversation—and my thoughts—above the waist.

In the dining room, Eliza leaned back in her chair with a thump. "I have to do this horrible physics assignment on electric potential and displacement currents and other stupid stuff I'm never going to need for the rest of my life."

He sat beside her. "Okay, one thing at a time."

The kitchen overlooked the dining area. It was the closest the house came to being open plan, so I started chopping up vegetables for our dinner while they worked.

Eliza pointed to her papers and laptop and explained her problem. As far as I could tell, they were barely speaking English.

"I think I can see where your problem lies," Austin said. "We need to go back to basics. Ohms Law."

She groaned. Such a teenager. Followed by some

protests. Austin ignored her, grabbed a piece of paper and started scribbling and explaining because, apparently, Ohms Law was the basis for a lot of electronics.

Eventually, Eliza started nodding, then mumbled something and told Austin to hold on while she did some calculations, her tone becoming more positive until eventually, I heard the magic words.

"I did it!"

Finally it was safe so I wandered over. One thing had been puzzling me. "Were you guys talking about some faraway cage?"

"That's a Faraday cage," Austin said. "I'd explain it to you but I don't think you'd find it very interesting."

I smiled. "Ha! And I thought it sounded poetic for something that's scientific."

"You're thinking of *The Faraway Tree*." Eliza smiled. "The kids' books."

"Maybe."

A pang shot through me because the two of them seemed to be a hundred miles ahead of me, discussing things I'd never understand. Which was fine for Eliza. I wanted her to get ahead. But that put Austin in a different league completely. Far, far away from me.

He turned to Eliza. "You said you were never going to need this stuff but you never know when it might come in handy."

She gave him the disbelieving teenager look. "Really? Like, when?"

"I'm a musician so you'd think that was all creative and had nothing to do with electrical theory?"

"Yep."

"Well, I knew a guy who plugged his amp into the

wrong impedance cabinet and blew up the speakers. He had to borrow an amp from another guy to play the gig and then he had to pay to get the thing repaired. So this isn't necessarily 'stupid stuff' and you never know when you might need it."

She looked down. "Well, first I have to pass the exam."

He ruffled her hair and stood. "You'll pass."

He joined me in the kitchen while I fried up onions in the pan. "Is that my payment?"

"Payment?"

"For my physics and electronics expertise. It's only fair."

I smiled. "I hoped you might stay. I've already chopped up extra chicken."

"Great, what are we having?"

"Chicken and bean burritos."

"Sounds good. Maybe you could whip up a cocktail for me to have while I'm waiting."

I grabbed a beer from the fridge, took off the lid, and shoved it into his hands. "There's your cocktail!"

He took a swig. "Best damn cocktail I ever had."

To his credit, he also asked if he could help, but I already had the meal under control as I mixed in the spices and added the final ingredients at the stove.

"I'm pretty good in the kitchen," he said.

I glanced at the sink. "Are you any good with plumbing? Faucets?"

Austin nodded toward the rusted faucet. "I think that thing is past it. I might be able to help, though."

"You've already been a great help with Eliza."

He came up behind me while I ground fresh black

pepper over the simmering burrito filling. His hands on my waist made me feel delicate, his breath on my neck sending a sizzle up my spine. I could get used to this. If only my life could always be this way.

I thought about Eliza in the next room. I was always thinking about her.

He took in the aroma. "You're obviously a good cook. Where did you learn?"

I moved away, set the plates on the counter on the dining room side. "Believe me, I didn't get it from my mother."

He was about to ask another question but I got in first. "Eliza, can you clear the table? Dinner's nearly ready."

No complaints from her. She knew when she was onto a good thing and carried her laptop and a pile of books to her room.

I turned to Austin. "The only thing I learned from my mom was what *not* to do. I was a teenager and probably could have survived on cereal, chips, and chocolate, but Eliza was little and needed taking care of. I learned to cook because I had to."

There were other things I'd had to learn too. How to clean up after Mom had vomited her guts up. How to get Eliza ready for school because Mom was too stoned. How to fight off her drunk boyfriends. Lots of fun stuff. Maybe I'd learned a lot from my mom after all.

"So you started cooking nutritious meals for her?" Austin asked.

"Yeah, I only wish we'd had all those recipes on YouTube back then. That's where I get all my tips now."

"Ever thought about opening up your own restaurant?"

"Only my own bar." The words slipped out.

Silence, then, "You want to own your own bar?"

"I didn't say that."

"Yes, you did."

I put the tortillas in the microwave, turned off the heat on the stove, and tipped the burrito mix into a serving bowl. Tried to ignore him. Couldn't. He'd caught me out.

"I told you I want a bar manager job. That part is true. And, yeah, maybe I do want to own my bar one day but that's just a dream. I can barely make ends meet as it is. But, hey, a girl can dream, can't she?"

Thoughtful, Austin nodded. Eliza stomped back into the room—she'd never been one to pitter patter—and set the table. She was good like that, always did whatever needed to be done.

Dinner was a success if I did say so myself. We often had one or two of Eliza's friends over for a meal but it didn't have quite this sophistication level, especially not with Michaela's self-centered conversation and her miraculous ability to disappear when it was time to clean up.

Tonight, Eliza talked about school but we talked about other things too, music, songwriting, and I shared some anecdotes about people who'd come into the bar.

After we'd finished eating, Austin pulled out his phone.

Eliza pointed. "Hey, not allowed!"

He frowned. "Sorry?"

"No phones at the table. If my friends and I aren't allowed, then neither are you."

Austin looked at me.

I shrugged. "It's true. I don't have many rules but

that's one of them. Dinner is for eating and conversation."

He held his phone out. "So you don't want me to order Peppe's for dessert?"

Eliza's eyes widened. "We can make an exception."

"Sure can," I added.

After cleaning up, we ate ice cream on the sofa in the living room, then Eliza said she was off to her room to finish studying.

Austin stood at the same time, picking up the empty bowls from the table. "You've finished your physics now, haven't you? There's nothing else you need help with?"

She rolled her eyes. "I'm not stupid, you know. I won't disturb you two."

Great. I was the adult, so how did I end up feeling like the teenager who was being caught out with her boyfriend?

Austin came back from the kitchen and settled on the sofa beside me. I'd been so happy when I'd found the vintage club sofa and matching chairs because they were stylish and a bargain to boot. Then there was Grandma's chair, which wasn't so stylish but it was as if a part of her was still in the room with us. And it was staying that way.

But I had something on my mind. "I don't want things to get too hot between us while Eliza's around."

"No problem. You want to set a good example."

"Exactly."

He slid his hand onto my thigh. "Eliza's not around."

I slapped his hand away. "I'll get us some beers."

Maybe that'd cool him down a little. I'd let him sidle up next to me in the kitchen. I probably shouldn't have done that either.

I kept my private life private when it came to Eliza. I'd lived with a guy in upstate New York and she knew about that, but somehow things changed for me when I came back to Frankston. The boyfriend situation, for one thing. Turned out Daniel hadn't been heartbroken that I was moving out of our shared apartment to live on the other side of the country. So I'd told myself I didn't care much either.

I'd dated a few guys since I'd been living here with Eliza. Nothing serious. Guys didn't seem to get serious with girls like me, which was probably why none of those relationships lasted.

Back in the living room, I handed Austin his beer, tucked my feet under my butt as I sat beside him. Close but not too close because I knew how easily it'd be to forget where we were and end up doing something stupid like having sex on the sofa where Eliza could walk in. That was not going to happen.

Changing to a sensible topic of conversation could only be a good thing so I said, "Thanks for helping Eliza with her homework."

"Glad I could help. She seems very diligent with her schoolwork."

"Yep, much more than I ever was."

I still wasn't sure if Eliza would make it to college, if she could get a scholarship, because paying for tuition was so far out of my reach it wasn't funny.

Austin gulped back some beer. "So where does she get it from?"

"No idea. Maybe I've given her some stability in her life. I'd like to think so. Or maybe it's just down to the fact my little sister is amazing."

"With the minor exception of the vomiting episode the other night."

My shoulders dropped. "Yeah, there was that."

I boasted some more about Eliza's grades and the awards she'd received at school. Glowed on the inside like a proud mother. Felt as if Austin was sharing in this with me. I felt so close to him that it made me wonder what it was like when you could share things like this with someone, the life experiences, the highs and lows.

He pressed a kiss to my lips. "You know one thing I like about you?"

I smiled at him dreamily. "Only one thing?"

"You don't care that I play with The Merchants of Menace."

"Yes, I do. The Merchants are a great band. I couldn't date you if you played in a band I hated, some horrible heavy metal band where you had lots of hair and wore studded leather."

"What I meant was, you're not impressed by the whole rock band thing and by the fame."

He didn't add 'by the money' but I was sure that was in there too. "Well, I'm not a groupie."

"No, you're not." He sidled closer. "You're something else, Tara Coleman."

Cupping my jaw in his hands, he placed a gentle kiss on my lips. He was close, so close, and I liked him this way.

"Maybe there's some other homework I can help you with." He peppered little kisses on my neck, made me feel delicate and wanted, made me feel like a teenager again.

I giggled at the warmth between us, at his suggestion. "You're not going to offer to help me with human biology, are you? That'd be tacky."

"I'm not going to offer anything. I'm going to take."

He reached for my hand and stood, pulling me up with him. "You don't have to do it all yourself, you know."

"Do what?"

"Everything. Life. Looking after Eliza."

Yes, I did. I always did everything myself, worked, paid the bills, organized the house, raised Eliza as best as I could.

Until tonight. Tonight I'd asked Austin for his help. Hadn't even thought anything of it because it had seemed the natural thing to do, but this wasn't natural for me.

I was always in control. Always did what I had to do. Never flinched, no matter how much things might hurt on the inside. That was another thing I'd learned from my mother or, rather, from her boyfriends. Never show fear.

Nerves simmered in my stomach because something was changing, turning, twisting deep inside me.

And whatever was happening, I was letting it.

CHAPTER SEVEN

Austin

I'd liked it better at my place when Tara had walked down the hallway naked but that wasn't happening tonight. She'd be naked all right—I'd make sure of that—just not in the hallway where her little sister might come out.

Tara slipped inside her bedroom and turned on the light, the door clicking closed behind us. Simple furniture, a big bed with a purple comforter and a padded headboard, a closet that took up most of one wall, ready-to-assemble by the look of it, and an antique chest of drawers.

She hadn't stayed at my place the other night. She'd run away. No way would I let her run away this time. She couldn't when we were at her house. Nowhere to run.

But she could kick me out. The thought made my gut clench because I was desperate for her to want me the way I longed for her.

"Too bright." Tara switched off the light and strode across to the window where she pulled the drapes open.

It took my eyes a moment to adjust, then I took in Tara's womanly form silhouetted against the window, a full moon glowing behind her. Yep, moonlight would do just fine.

I ambled to the window, swept her into my arms, and tossed her on the bed. She shrieked, then covered her mouth, embarrassed. She didn't want to make too much noise. Fine by me. We didn't have to make a racket to enjoy ourselves.

My eyes were on Tara. I couldn't get them off her. Her lips were parted, dark hair splayed across the pillow, that magnificent body laid across the bed. For me. All for me.

I kicked off my shoes, ripped off my shirt, and lay beside her. The kisses came hard and fast, hands wandering, mine and hers. Too many clothes. I helped her out of hers, tossing them to the floor so she was naked, just the way I liked her. Kept kissing her, my mouth on hers, on her neck, her pretty little shoulders, her nipples.

"Mine, all mine," I whispered the words.

She nudged me away. "We do this my way."

My way, her way, any way was fine by me.

She pushed me back, got on top, kissed my chest, then trailed lower, her fingers on the button and zipper of my jeans. I lifted my ass while she pulled the rest of my clothing off. Such a wonderful feeling, her little hands on my body.

As ready as I'd ever been, I rolled her over but she groaned and pushed me back so she was on top again.

"My way."

That was when I found out her way was torture, absolute fucking torture. She was licking and teasing, brushing against me, gently at first. She barely let me touch her, slapping my hand away, while she ran her fingers and tongue all over me. Teasing me. Driving me crazy till I was ready to explode.

Followed by the beautiful moment when she finally reached for a condom from the top drawer. This was what I'd been waiting for. She let me enter her. And torture turned to the most amazing experience of my life. Tara was breathing faster, not there yet. I held back, waited, heard her moan, then let myself go. Felt my body shatter into a thousand pieces.

And if there was anyone to pick up the pieces, it was Tara.

We talked. We rolled around on the bed. Went at it again. Chatted a little. It made me feel closer to her.

My arms around her, I looked into her pale eyes, eyelids that were heavy. She was getting sleepy. Perhaps I'd worn her out. Surprising it wasn't the other way around.

"You'll have to go soon," she whispered.

"Soon," I lied.

I wasn't going anywhere. I stroked her hair, told her she was beautiful, because she was. Told her how she'd taken my breath away from the first moment I saw her. How she'd made a big impression by pushing Nick around when he and Lachie had tried to trash the band room. Told her how comfortable I felt around her, how much I liked Eliza too, how I'd been happy to help the two of them that night.

Tara's eyes were closed, her breathing rhythmic. Asleep.

I closed my eyes too.

CHAPTER EIGHT

Tara

Movement by the edge of the bed, the shuffle of footsteps, the rustle of the comforter. My eyes sprung open. It was morning.

And Austin was leaning over the bed, giving me a kiss on the cheek. He was dressed, wasn't in bed, shouldn't have been in bed, not if it was morning. My head fuzzy, I couldn't quite get things straight.

Then it hit me. Austin, fully dressed, at the side of my bed.

I sat up, the sheet falling to my waist. I looked down. I was naked, my boobs on display, nothing he hadn't seen before.

Another kiss, on the lips this time, a smile on his face. Maybe that kiss knocked some sense into me because suddenly I felt very awake. Something else I felt, a knot deep in my stomach.

"You were asleep," he said.

"I know."

That was the whole problem. I'd fallen asleep last night and had no one to blame other than myself. I felt like

Rip Van Winkle, the old guy who woke up to find it was twenty years later and the world had changed. I could feel it, a fissure in the fabric of time, something deep inside me because this wasn't the way I'd planned it.

I glanced at the bedside clock. "That's not very rock 'n' roll."

He edged down onto the bed. "What?"

"Getting up this early. I thought you guys were supposed to party all night and sleep all day, then get up for another round of booze and women."

"Maybe I'm not very rock 'n' roll. I heard footsteps in the hallway so I got up. It was Eliza, saying she was getting some headache pills. I remembered there was that Swiss bakery near the highway, so I asked her if she liked croissants and if they might help her headache."

"I'm surprised you didn't offer her more ice cream for breakfast."

He shrugged. "I didn't think of it. They're still warm."

"What are?"

"The croissants."

"And—don't tell me—you're making coffee?"

"No, Eliza is."

I nudged him off the bed, swung my legs around, and wondered what to wear. Austin was standing there, a satisfied smile on his face and a gleam in his eyes as he looked down at me.

"Out, out!" I shoved him out of the door so I could get dressed on my own and get my head together.

Now I knew what people meant when they talked about the morning after the night before. So unsettling. It wasn't as if he was the first guy I'd had sex with. When I was younger, I'd woken up in all kinds of strange places, at friends' houses, after parties, but it had never been like this.

Clothes, I needed clothes, so I put on a striped T-shirt and black pedal pushers, then took a deep breath, and I was out of there.

As I strode into the dining room, my world turned to slow motion, my legs suddenly heavy, my life going at half-speed. Eliza was passing the coffee mugs over the counter to Austin, the two of them chatting, the table set with plates and croissants. This was too weird for words. As if I'd accidentally walked into someone else's life.

"Morning, Sis."

Eliza's voice. My world shifted back to regular speed and I had to switch back to regular Tara.

"How's your head, honey?" I asked.

"Heaps better." She joined Austin at the table. "Just the thought of croissants did it to me."

"I'm sure the ibuprofen helped too."

"Well, *duh*."

Yep, my little sister was back to normal. I sat down gingerly, unsure of what might happen next, but there was nothing to worry about. The croissants were good, better than good. In fact, breakfast was spectacular.

"When is your physics assignment due?" Austin asked.

Eliza sipped her coffee. "Today."

"Nothing like leaving things till the last minute."

"Well, I didn't, not really. I started it ages ago and then couldn't get my head around it. Sooo glad I've got it finished now."

Austin pushed his empty plate away. "Do you need a ride to school?"

"In your car?" Her eyes widened, her whole face

lighting up. It was one of the things I liked about Eliza, the way she didn't hold back.

"Well, yes, in my car, unless you'd prefer going by bicycle."

She piled up the plates, took them to the kitchen. "No, the Thunderbird will do just fine. I hope the top's off. Then everyone will be able to see me."

"The top's on. It's staying on."

"Spoil sport!"

"As it happens, I love the hard top with the opera window." He raised his eyebrows. "So do you want a ride or not?"

"I'll brush my teeth and grab my bag. Be right back."

She left. The two of them seemed like a happy family already, which wasn't how this was meant to be. This was one of the things I tried to protect Eliza from, the disappointment if a relationship didn't work out. She had her own life and friends to deal with and didn't need to be burdened by mine too.

I cleared my throat, tried to sound normal. "Got much going on today?"

Austin nodded. "Not a lot but a few things. I'm meeting a friend for lunch, a guy I studied with who's practicing here in Frankston."

"Practicing what?"

"Architecture."

I forced a smile to my face. "Sorry, I'm not properly awake yet."

Warmth spread to my cheeks. It showed how different our lives were. My friends had regular jobs. They worked. They didn't 'practice'.

"I need to catch up with Nick too, though maybe not

today," he added.

He wasn't the only one who needed to talk to Nick. I wouldn't be doing it today either but soon I had to put myself forward as a potential bar manager. It'd be more responsibility and that meant more money.

"What's up with your rock star singer?" I asked.

He raised his eyebrows. "That wasn't sarcasm I heard, was it?"

"Maybe just a little. Sorry, I should have more respect. That job puts food on the table for us."

"Except in the case of croissants."

"Which were amazing, thank you so much. You've set the bar high. I think Eliza was impressed too."

At which moment she swept into the room, her backpack slung over one shoulder.

"Ready whenever you are," she said.

Austin stood. "Sure."

I got up too, my hand on Eliza's arm. "Can I have a quick word first?"

"Go for it," she said.

Then, an uncomfortable moment as Austin looked from Eliza to me. "Okay, I'll meet you outside."

"Thanks for everything," I said, then realized what 'everything' encapsulated. "I mean, for the croissants."

He smiled, amused at my momentary awkwardness, then kissed me on the lips.

"See you in a sec," he said to Eliza, then left.

I wasn't sure about kissing in front of Eliza, wasn't sure about anything, and that was the whole problem. Not that I was being coy. Eliza was sixteen years old, not a kid anymore, and it was pretty obvious I'd been around. But I didn't want to throw my sex life in her face and simply hope for the best.

She turned to me. "Yep."

"I need to be straight with you. It's obvious Austin and I have started seeing each other."

"Yeah?"

"And I like him a lot but I don't want that to affect our relationship. Look, I've had boyfriends before. You know that." I swallowed the lump in my throat. "I don't even know how to say this. I'm not like Mom. I'm not a drug addict."

Some small part—or maybe a large part—of me was afraid of that very thing, that I was my mother's daughter, that if I didn't watch myself I'd end up just like her. Most of the time, that fear was a niggling inside me and then there were times it was a stab through the lungs that would stop me from breathing. Because I couldn't end up that way. I couldn't.

Eliza slipped her backpack off her shoulder. "I know that."

"So, things won't be changing between us. I won't be bringing home a different guy every night. You'll always be safe here and I'll always take care of you."

"Tara, it's not that big a deal." Sometimes my little sister sounded like a grown woman. "I know you've had boyfriends before, that Daniel guy for one. Who sounded like a bit of jerk if you ask me, but that's just my opinion."

"You might be right there."

Not an admission I'd made before because when I'd come back two years ago, Eliza had been too young to understand. She was older now.

"And I know you've dated other guys since you came back to Frankston," she added. "I don't expect you to be a nun."

"Good." I folded my arms. This wasn't good at all. "Glad we've got that clear."

"And Austin isn't just 'a guy'. I can tell he's special."

My stomach rumbled with fear. "How can you possibly tell?"

"Oh, puh-lease, I'm not a little kid anymore. It's pretty obvious. He's the only guy you've let stay the night."

I pressed a hand to my temple, swallowed the nerves in my throat. As if I didn't already know. As if I hadn't just worked that out. I needed some space so I could get used to the idea. Surely that wasn't too much to ask, except Eliza hadn't finished yet.

"And it's about time. Honestly, I was wondering what was going on with you. My friends have moms who are divorced and they all have boyfriends stay over. This is the twenty-first century. Sometimes I think you're stuck in the 1950s."

"No, it's just…"

"I know what you're going to say. Just the clothes. And the music. Look, I like the clothes. You've got your own thing going and I'm glad you've got this thing happening with Austin. Finally."

I had a funny feeling I was getting the mother-daughter talk from my little sister, which was wrong in so many ways I didn't even know where to start.

I straightened, tried to maintain some decorum. "I didn't plan for it to happen this way. Or I'd have talked to you first."

She picked up her backpack. "I don't know what you're going on about. I've been waiting for this to happen. I mean, it was always going to be hard for me to ask to have a boy stay over if you didn't have boyfriends staying the night."

Panic shot through me. "Boy? What boy?"

Eliza rolled her eyes. "There's no one *now* but that doesn't mean there won't be. Of course I'm going to want to have my boyfriend stay over when I get one. Honestly, all my friends' older sisters have boyfriends stay over. It's not that big a deal and I'm glad you're finally getting with the program."

I sighed. "Um, don't you have to go to school now?"

"Yeah." She slung her backpack over one shoulder. "And *you* were the one holding me up."

Looking thoroughly exasperated, she kissed me on the cheek and got on her way.

I leaned against the countertop, let out a long sigh. Tried to ignore the fluttering in my stomach, couldn't ignore the pang in my chest, because now my heart was overtaking my brain.

I'd always made such a point of being in control all the time. Not anymore. Things had gone way too far for that. This wasn't just sex. Austin wasn't just a guy. This was something else completely.

Cupid's arrow? Was there really such a thing?

I was in big trouble.

CHAPTER NINE

Austin

Tara looked amazing with that red checkered shirt tied at the waist, showing a hint of the creamy skin of her midriff. She'd put the red lipstick back on so you'd never know anything was going on with her.

I'd got to The Swamp early for our meeting, not that it was hard to keep ahead of Nick, and had dragged Tara into the back room. She hadn't put up much resistance. I hadn't pushed things, just enjoyed holding her in my arms and kissing her, hence the need to fix her lipstick.

She didn't want to let on to Nick that we were seeing each other, not yet, because she was still getting used to the idea. Hell, I'd gotten used to it within the first five minutes. I didn't argue, though. Nick was her boss, this was her job, and it meant a lot to her.

Also, I had bigger things on my mind. The moment of truth. Time to tell Nick I was leaving the band.

Even though I knew this was the right thing to do— the right thing for me—anxiety simmered in my stomach. Damn it, the guys and I had been through so much together, shared all kinds of weird experiences from being on the road, things only they could understand. I had to hope they'd understand this too.

Nick and I were at cross-purposes. I'd known that even before I got here.

"I don't get what you mean about flow," Nick said.

We were talking about bar design and architecture, which was definitely not his specialty area.

I got up from the stool. "I'll show you." We headed for the main entry. "Okay, pretend you're a thirsty guy looking for a beer or a girl to chat to. Pretend you're walking in here for the first time. What do you see?"

"The bar."

"And that's at the far end of the room. It's the middle of the day so the place is empty but imagine how hard it'd be to get a drink if the place was packed."

He nodded. "I see what you mean."

"The bar should be along this wall." I pointed to the side. "So it's the first thing you see when you walk in. It welcomes you into the space, creates a focal point, draws you in."

Nick mumbled approval.

"It also means that if people are sitting at the bar talking to each other, at least some of them will be facing the entry whereas now everyone has their back to the entrance. Not to mention which, Tara and the other bartenders can make eye contact with the patrons, make them feel comfortable right away."

"Ha! She doesn't make me feel comfortable."

"The customers like her, don't they?"

"They love her."

He hadn't noticed I'd mentioned Tara by name, not that it mattered. I had to change the subject, tell him what

I came here to tell him regardless of what he was after.

Nick headed back for the bar, motioned for me to join him. "So what do you think of the actual bar?"

I'd answer a couple of questions, then I'd tell him. I had to.

I ran my hand across the top of the bar. "This is a magnificent piece of mahogany. You wouldn't want to get rid of this. It could easily be incorporated into a refurbishment, along with the timber paneling at the front. Just look at it. Such a rich, warm color and the bits where people have scratched in their names only adds to the patina."

Nick grinned. "Hey, my bar top has patina!"

"But it all depends on whether you want to maintain the character of the place. It's not as if this is the Waldorf."

"So do you think your dad might be interested in taking on a job like this?"

"He might be."

I already knew Dad was interested. I was interested too. This could be a tidy little job to bring to my father's practice. When I joined him. I hadn't asked Dad yet, but that was a moot point because I knew he'd love to have me.

Ryan, an old friend from the first firm I'd worked at, had suggested the two of us join forces and branch out together. Two young guns. It was a good idea but I was sticking with my dad.

Then The Merchants would be part of my past. I couldn't do both. It was a hard call, *my* call because this was my life. My jaw tight, nerves rocketed through me.

Time to bite the bullet. It was hard, even despite my

certainty.

"Let's take a seat." I definitely wanted him to be sitting down for this.

He slid onto a barstool. "I see what you mean about people having their backs to the door."

"There's more, Nick."

"I'm sure there is. I'm finding out there's a lot more to the bar business than I thought."

"That's not what I meant. I'm glad you'd like my dad to design the new bar for you but that's not what I had in mind."

"What then?"

"I'd like to take on the job myself. I'm seriously interested and there are a few reasons for that."

This was a huge risk. I'd been out of architecture for a long time, so who even knew if I could make it? This was a competitive industry, maybe not as cutthroat as music, but still with a few top dogs holding onto their positions ruthlessly, the way my father did. I wasn't even sure I'd be able to get a foot back in without him.

Still, despite everything, I *felt* like an architect. It was what I'd been put on this earth to do. That was what it all came down to, what was inside me.

"Great idea." Nick nodded. "You could do this over the next six months while we're all in town. Before The Flats, that is, and before we line up anymore concerts."

"That's what I'm trying to tell you," I said. "I won't be doing anymore concerts. I've come back to Frankston for good. I want to settle back down here."

Nick smiled, didn't get it. "What do you mean?"

"I'm leaving the band, Nick."

The smile left his face, his brows furrow, eyes hooding

over. He got it now. "What the fuck are you talking about?"

"Look, this has been building for a while. It's not just one thing. It's a lot of things."

Snarling now. "Don't even try to tell me I'm one of those things."

"I'm not. This whole lifestyle is so crazy and it brings out the worst in people. There's this whole thing with Lachie's stalker for a start."

He shrugged it off. "For fuck's sake, no one's going to attack you in your sleep. We've been through this and we've got people keeping an eye on it."

That was part of the problem. We had people monitoring the situation. What kind of life was that? Besides, it wasn't exactly that I was worried for our personal safety, not yet anyway, but it just confirmed that this wasn't my world.

A sudden impulse shot through me, the urge to get away. Not out of the bar but to get far away, if only for a short time. Ironic, I knew, because I'd only just got here and this was the place I planned to stay. But it'd be good to escape for a bit, take Tara with me, enjoy each other's company.

I didn't dare look across at her, not yet. I had to get through this first.

Then the conversation I knew was coming, about how bad my timing was, and he was right. Nick brought up The Flats. Told me how pissed off he was and that he wasn't going to hide it. They'd get another bass player. The Merchants would go on.

"I can't talk to you right now, Austin," he said.

I got up. "We can talk later."

For a few minutes, it seemed he was calming down.

Until his parting words. "Fuck off out of here, dude."

My shoulders stiffened. Maybe I deserved that.

I glanced at Tara at the other end of the bar. She flicked her eyes toward the exit, a signal I hoped. When I reached the door, I looked back to see she was pouring Nick a beer with a bourbon chaser. This was typical of Nick. The guy drank way too much. I probably did when we were on the road too, only now I'd reached the end of that particular road and was better off away from it all.

That's exactly where I was going. Away.

CHAPTER TEN

Tara

I didn't know long Austin would be hanging around outside, but I was desperate to talk to him so I could find out what the hell was going on. Whatever had happened, that was some heavy shit. I'd only heard the last bit where Nick told him to fuck off, and that was enough.

Nick had looked like he needed a drink so I'd gotten him one. Didn't have to be a mind reader to work that out. I just wished he knew when to stop because he seemed to think it was a good idea to simply keep on drinking.

I leaned against the bar, clenched my teeth, told myself not to do anything stupid. Another drunk bar owner, that was all I needed.

Damn it, this job was important to me. Even if I didn't make it to bar manager, I still needed the money I was earning now. The tips too. I didn't just have myself to think about. Eliza and I needed to eat, pay the bills, buy clothes and school books.

A spark of frustration flickered inside me. It was easy for him with so much money he could buy the place on a whim. Easy for him because it didn't matter to him whether he worked or not. No problem for Nick because when the going got tough, he got drunk.

I couldn't lose another job because of a lazy drunken owner. I couldn't. I drummed my fingers on the bar.

Deep breaths, Tara. Take it easy. You can keep your big mouth shut, you can do it.

No, I couldn't. Screw the deep breaths. The little spark inside me exploded into flames, anger burning deep in my gut. I held myself back, relatively speaking, as I laid it on the line for Nick. If I looked cool on the outside, that was an illusion because it'd only take one small thing to set me off.

Then the words I couldn't believe were coming out of my mouth.

"You've got to stop drinking. You need to get your shit together."

From me, the barmaid, to my boss. What had I done? What was I thinking?

I held his gaze, didn't waver, despite the fact my insides were churning, jaw clenched, tendons in my neck straining. Shit, I'd done it again, gone too far, and my job was on the line.

Still, despite my doubts and desperation, I would never show fear. The one thing I'd learned from my mother's boyfriends. I couldn't back down. I didn't.

Then I saw what Nick hadn't seen, Lily walking in the door. It was instinct. I couldn't help myself as I tried to warn him, tried not to look too obvious.

Hell, I didn't even know what was going on with those two. They'd been in a relationship before or at least I hoped they had because they had a child together. Maybe they'd had some sort of long distance thing going on while

The Merchants were touring or maybe they'd broken up. Whatever had happened in the past, there was definitely something going on now.

I gave Lily a sympathetic smile because anyone who was seeing Nick deserved my sympathy.

Then I got them each two glasses of water. I hoped he'd take the hint and stick to water but you could never tell with guys like him. In fact, I was sure he wouldn't take the hint. I had a feeling he was too thick when it came to women, and his senses were already dulled with alcohol.

So I leaned close to him and whispered, "Play it nice or she'll throw it in your face."

He laughed. I was deadly serious, doing him a favor, and he laughed. What nerve.

I'd had more than enough so I left them to it. Lily was going to need all the luck she could get dealing with Nick, and meanwhile, I had to hope Austin was still waiting for me.

I had a quick word with the other bartender who'd just started her shift, told her I was on a break. I should never have let my temper get the better of me, should never have wasted so much time talking to Nick, not if Austin was outside, which I hoped he was.

First thing I did was check the messages on my phone, relieved to find he was parked nearby, waiting for me.

My heart skipped a beat when I saw him leaning against the door of his Thunderbird, arms folded, long legs crossed at the ankles, dark hair slicked back. What a duo—the coolest car ever produced with the hunkiest man there was. Waiting for me. The sort of guy I never even imagined I could find. It took my breath away.

I ran into his arms and he caught me, spun me around,

made me feel like a delicate little thing. Pressing my lips against his I kissed him, a chaste kiss, but loaded with emotion because I was bubbling over to see him.

Happiness. Was this what it felt like?

He held me at arm's length. "Where can we go? A café, my place?"

"I'm on a break and don't have much time." I leaned against the car. "What happened with Nick? That looked like a heavy conversation. Is everything all right?"

"Yes and no."

"O-okay, which bit is yes and which bit is no?"

"I told Nick I was leaving the band."

My mouth fell open. "When did you decide all this?"

"It's been brewing for awhile."

I blinked. "You're leaving the band?"

He must've seen the shock in my face because he reached for my arm and stroked it. This was supposed to be reassuring. Instead it felt like the earth was shifting beneath my feet.

What else was going on? What else hadn't he told me about?

"That's a bit of a bombshell." I choked the words out.

"Yeah, it is. Sorry about that."

"When were you going to tell me about this?"

"Well, I'm telling you now."

Resentment burned at the back of my throat. Sure, this was his life and his decision and maybe nothing to do with me, but it hurt. Because I wanted to be part of his life, wanted him to confide in me, to share the good things and the bad.

Instead it felt like I was an 'extra' in his life, a girl who wandered on set and wasn't vital to this production, the sort of girl who was a dime a dozen. There were plenty of women like me and didn't I know it.

I pressed a hand to my temple. "I can't believe this."

He went through it all with me, the way he'd always felt like the odd man out in the band, how the songs he wrote often got sidelined, how he'd been thinking about this for a while. Some of this I'd heard before and some I hadn't. He had a weird story about a girl wanting to give him a blowjob in the middle of the night and how that had freaked him out. An even weirder story about Lachie having a stalker who seemed to be somehow getting closer to the band.

Despair settled deep in my gut while he spilled his guts to me, not because I thought he was making the wrong decision about leaving the band but because he hadn't included me in any way, shape, or form. I had no idea why he hadn't told me any of this earlier, hadn't even mentioned it.

"So, am I the last to find out?" I asked.

"It's not like that. I wanted to speak to Nick first. I wasn't going tell anyone until I'd spoken to the guys first. I haven't even spoken to Lachie and Cooper yet."

"They don't know?"

"Not yet."

Somehow that didn't make me feel any better. Damn it, I wanted a man I could rely on, someone dependable and sturdy, not someone who did things without me. 'Musician' wasn't exactly a reliable profession but at least I'd known where I stood with that. And now he was shifting the ground from under my feet.

"I haven't told my dad yet either," he added. "I need to speak to him too."

"Because the two of you are close?"

"That and more. He's always wanted me join his firm and now I'm ready to settle back in town with a regular job."

"As an architect?"

He nodded. "This is the right thing for me."

Another thing he hadn't included me in.

It was more than that though, much more. My chest tightened, my stomach clenching into a knot. This should've been good news but it wasn't going down well, and it wasn't just Austin's timing.

I was never going to be an architect's girlfriend or partner, never going to be his equal, nowhere near it. Somehow I knew deep inside that I might've had a better chance with him as the bass player than him as a professional architect, even with a band as big as The Merchants. A girl like me was much more acceptable in his musical world. Bands, bars, parties, it all seemed to fit.

An architect, though, that was someone who existed in a different sphere from mine, someone who was educated and had a profession, who mixed with certain kinds of people, who went to bars to find a drink, not a partner.

Maybe I'd been fooling myself all along. I felt it. The beginning of the end.

"You seem put out," he said.

I opened my mouth to speak, wasn't sure where to start. "I'm in shock, I guess. I didn't see this coming."

"You'll get used to the idea."

"Will I?"

His eyes narrowed. "I hope you're not…"

"Not what?"

"A lot of women are only interested in the guy in the

band, the glamor, and fame."

His brown eyes that could be so warm filled with accusation. He'd come out with it so we might as well clear the air.

I jabbed a finger in his chest. "Yeah, well, not me. I'm not waiting for some rock star knight in shining armor to rescue me from the bar. So don't look at me that way."

He had it the wrong way around and I couldn't even begin to explain. His upbringing might not have been perfect but it was a far cry from mine. He'd never been in my shoes, never had to shift from town to town and start all over again, never struggled to put food on the table, never had to wonder if it was time to call the paramedics for his mother who was drugged out of her mind.

His gaze softened. "I thought you'd be excited. It means I'm staying right here in Frankston, not just for six months while the band's cutting the record, but for a long time. The foreseeable future. That's a good thing, isn't it? For us."

I clasped my hands together to stop them from trembling. "It is. It's wonderful having you around."

And it was. But guys moved on. It happened all the time. It had certainly happened with every other guy I'd known.

"You don't look very happy." He took my hand into his. "You're shaking."

"I'm in shock. It's a lot to take in."

It was a lot more than shock. This was love. It had crept up on me, this gradual swelling, this tenderness. The passion between us—I knew all about that—but love was on another level.

There was no other explanation. God knows, if this

was any other guy, that temper of mine would've taken over and I'd have told him in no uncertain terms to shove it.

But, no, it wasn't love. How could I have thought that even for a moment?

My eyes filled with tears. This wasn't like me. Something was taking over inside and I didn't know what to do.

Austin pulled me close, mumbled words of affection, rubbed my back. His chest felt so safe and secure that I didn't care if this was an illusion. I let the first tears fall, then forced myself to be strong. Because if I didn't take care of myself, no one else would.

I edged away, leaned against the car beside him, my arms crossed. "Guess I won't be talking to Nick about that bar manager position just yet, then."

"I wouldn't talk to him about anything today."

"No, it's pretty obvious he's pissed."

It felt as if yet another chance was slipping through my fingers. I still had to approach Nick at the first possible opportunity, whenever that might be. It wasn't that I expected privileges because I was seeing Austin but I did expect a level playing field. No such luck.

Austin stepped across to stand in front of me, taking my hands into his. "You know what we need? To get away. Just the two of us."

"But this is my home."

"I'm not talking about getting away for a long time. A short break, just two or three nights."

I still didn't quite believe it. This sort of thing didn't happen to people like me. This wasn't *Pretty Woman*.

"That'd be nice," I mumbled.

"How about New York? It's far enough away that we can really feel like we've gone somewhere."

It still wasn't sinking in. "I don't know. I'll have to think about it."

Then there were the words I stopped myself from saying—*I have responsibilities, you know.* I couldn't leave at the drop of a hat and abandon Eliza. She relied on me.

I bit my lip. I didn't want to sound like that person, the responsible one who knew better, the one who never had any fun. Didn't want to *be* that person. And it wasn't as if I'd signed up for being a parent, not yet anyway.

"You're thinking about Eliza?" he asked.

"Yes."

"Sixteen is old enough for her to be on her own for a couple of days." As I opened my mouth to argue, he held a hand out. "But you're the boss so whatever you say goes. And Eliza could always come with us if she had to."

He must have seen the confusion in my face because he added, "That came out all wrong. I've got something more romantic in mind, just the two of us, but if it can't be that way, I'd be happy to have Eliza along too. It's all on me. You don't need to worry about the money. As long as you're there, that's the part that matters to me."

This was getting harder to argue with, and I didn't even know why I'd want to disagree with such a fabulous idea. What was the matter with me?

I bit my lip to stop myself from doing something dumb like getting teary again and nodded. Because I wanted this. I wanted him. I wanted it all.

He wrapped his arms around me and for those moments, it felt like we might just have something deep, certainly deeper than anything that had come before, a relationship that might last.

Despite this, something niggled inside. My mind was having trouble going back to the start where he told me he was leaving the band. Then I worked it out. I could be a bit slow sometimes.

I knew what was bothering me. He hadn't trusted me.

CHAPTER ELEVEN

Austin

A lot had gone down in the last few days. It felt like everything was happening at once and maybe that was how it had to be.

I'd booked our tickets to New York for the weekend—just me and Tara, I was pleased to say. We'd been spending a lot of time together, hanging out at her place and going out, and it felt right. As if this was how things were meant to be.

Then there was the hard part. I'd talked to the other guys straight after speaking to Nick. Cooper had taken the news better than I thought he would, whereas Lachie had taken it worse. A lot worse. I didn't even want to think about it.

Now I was back at The Swamp with Nick, the two of us at a table down the back. I seemed to be spending a lot of time here.

I'd been calling both him and Lily after their boy, Thomas, slipped in the bath and hit his head. That was bigger than me leaving the band, and maybe it had put events into perspective for Nick because he seemed to be used to the idea that I'd left the band.

The main thing was that Thomas was on the mend but somehow Nick seemed to think he was to blame when the accident was down to a moment's inattention, nothing more, at a time when the kid was clowning around in the bath. It was strange Nick should shoulder so much responsibility for something that wasn't his fault when there were so many times he'd acted like an idiot and absolved himself of all responsibility. A loveable idiot nonetheless.

Also I could tell something else was going on—between him and Lily. I'd always sensed it was a one-sided relationship but it seemed Nick had finally seen what had been in front of his eyes all along because Lily was a wonderful woman. I told him I hadn't known about the two of them.

"Not a lot of people did," he said.

Did. The past tense. I saw it in his eyes and worked it out. He and Lily had gotten back together. And split up again. The poor guy must be shattered.

It sounded like Lily blamed him for Thomas's accident, which didn't seem fair. There were plenty of other things she could blame Nick for, but not that. I put my arm around him in the hope it might help him feel better. Told him I was sorry. Because I was. Wished I could offer him more than just moral support.

I asked where Tara was, only to find out it was her day off. She'd already told me and I'd forgotten. I was aching to tell Nick we were seeing each other but figured I could keep my mouth shut a bit longer. Tara wanted to talk to him first and I didn't want to stand in her way.

Nick and I wandered around, taking a look at the bar,

talking about his vision for the place. He seemed to want to get down to business, which was not a side of him I'd seen before. He was very good at the music and songwriting business, for sure, but this was different.

After a while I asked, "So the band room can stay?"

"Definitely."

"I'm glad you said that. Problem is, the sound is shit."

"Yeah, it is."

He couldn't argue because he sure as hell knew this was true. It was a rectangular room with hard surfaces so the sound bounced off the back wall from the stage, which meant there were sound waves going all over the place. Not what you wanted.

"I'm not suggesting a major refurbishment," I said. "If there are bands playing, the place doesn't need to look like something out of *Architectural Digest*."

That made him smile.

I kept going. "Nothing wrong with a big empty room you can fill with people. You'll need some acoustic paneling along the back wall in particular. The stuff comes in funky shapes that'll fit with the vibe of the room."

"Sounds good."

And maybe I could play here after I got that rockabilly outfit together. Small gigs would suit me fine. I had plenty of songs and a guitar player in mind, but this wasn't the time to mention that.

A pang cut through me. Because The Merchants had been such a big part of my life and now I'd be going from playing stadiums to gigs with fifty people. The band was a big loss to me, I couldn't deny it. And I had to move on.

I cleared my throat. "You might want to set up a memorabilia wall."

His eyes lit up. "Great idea."

"Wouldn't be hard to do, not between the crap that the previous owner left behind and some Merchants' collectibles. It'd be a great talking point for people who might get there early."

Nick was nodding. Listening too. He was seriously interested.

I forced myself to focus. "The bar is the big problem, though."

"How?"

"There's no bar access in the band room."

He shrugged. "Yeah, people get their beers first, then head into the band room."

"And what happens when they get thirsty again? They have to leave the band room. You want to make it as easy as possible for them to buy more drinks and spend more money."

Realization in his eyes, he was starting to get the hang of this. "Yeah, you're right. So we need a second bar in the band room."

"Maybe not. If you do that, you'd need a dedicated staff member here whenever there's a band playing. It's also more expense, what with relocating the plumbing and all."

Frowning now. "How do you know all this shit?"

"You're in the bar business now. You have to learn all this 'shit' too." I pointed to the other side of the room. "It'd be easy enough to knock a hole in the wall and set up bar station down that end. You'd still have one big bar plus there'll be bar access into the band room."

"Cool."

"I'm glad you're taking this seriously."

"Of course I am."

This job meant a lot to me, partly because of the history of The Swamp and what it meant to the local band scene and partly because this was Nick's bar now.

It was more than that, though. I'd spoken to my father about taking him up on his offer of joining the firm. If the look on his face at the time was anything to go by, I was making him the happiest man in the world. Dad was always hard-nosed when it came to the business side of things and started asking about refurbishing The Swamp right away. Hadn't wasted any time.

When I first graduated, I'd refused to work for my father because I'd wanted to stand on my own two feet. I'd done that now, with a few years of architecture practice under my belt and a killer career in a band. I'd proven myself but that wasn't the end of it. This was only the beginning, a new beginning.

I was sticking with some of the things I knew, with my father, not with Ryan who wanted to start up our own practice together.

And with Tara. Big things were happening with her. I could feel it, a shift in the times, the ground swelling beneath my feet.

"Yep," I said. "The Times They Are A-Changin'."

Nick screwed up his nose. "I didn't think you were a Dylan fan."

"I'm not." I looked around the room. "He recorded that stuff back in the sixties and everything is still a-changin'. Not sure if that makes it poignant or trite."

Nick whacked me on the back. "You think too much."

"Something else I was thinking about … Tara, the bartender."

"What about her?"

"Nothing." I clammed up, shouldn't have said anything, wasn't quite sure why I'd come out with her name.

"That's not a 'nothing' look on your face."

I changed the subject. I'd leave the rest to Tara because her job was something she wanted to tackle on her own.

CHAPTER TWELVE

Tara

It had been a long time since I'd been nervous, or anywhere near it, at a job interview.

Sometimes a new job meant nothing more than a chat with the manager, but a few times I'd had to present my resume and sit through endless questions about my work experience, including a couple of doozies with case scenarios where I had to explain what I'd do under various circumstances. As if I didn't deal with drunks and all sorts of people every day of my life.

I remembered one interview that was a series of quiz questions on 101 different cocktail recipes. I hadn't been able to take the whole thing seriously because I'd felt like I was on an episode of *Jeopardy*. Was that show even still running?

What a waste of time that'd been. If they'd put me on the bar for ten minutes, it would have told them everything they'd needed to know.

Then, this wasn't a job interview, not exactly. I'd made an appointment to see Nick to discuss my role at the bar. So why were my nerve endings on edge?

I'd insisted we meet inside Nick's office. I wasn't sure he'd even known he had an office until I'd told him, the poor guy.

I closed the door behind us, shifted a pile of papers to the desk so I could sit on the chair while Nick ambled over to the side of the desk. This room was as much a dump as the rest of the place, which wasn't his fault but it was time to change things. And that was where I came in.

I smoothed down my skirt. I'd dressed for the occasion in a fitted red and black floral dress. This was my version of job interview clothes because I still had to be me.

"I could put your office in order if you wanted me to," I said.

"Oh, no, it's—" He looked around, embarrassed. "Actually, that might be a good idea."

"That's not why I came today, though."

He sat there, not a clue what to do. He reminded me of a little kid whose mother had forced him to shine his shoes and put on a tie for a special occasion. He was so far out of his league it wasn't funny. For a split second, I felt sorry for him.

I raised my eyebrows. "You don't like being in an office, do you? You'd rather be sitting at the bar. That's your sort of place."

He nodded. "You got that right."

"That's kind of why I'm here. Because this is the first bar you've ever owned and you don't really know what you're doing. This is all new to you and I think you might need some help running the place."

He twisted his lips, didn't say anything. My efforts at being tactful were way off the mark. Shit, I should have buttered him up more, pandered to his ego, instead of getting straight to the point. Maybe it wasn't too late.

"You're very good at what you do, the band, that is. You're a brilliant songwriter and front man, and you've forged an amazing career with The Merchants. There are thousands of struggling musicians out there and you've succeeded where so many others couldn't make it. I think you can be a great front man for The Swamp too. You've got what it takes, but a bar isn't a band. They're different and each one needs a distinctive approach."

"This isn't like you."

"Sorry?"

He leaned back in his chair. "So polite, so nice, all this beating around the bush. When you said I didn't know what I was doing, that sounded more like the Tara I know."

I gritted my teeth. He'd been around too, and could smell a fake a mile away. One thing I'd never been was a fake.

Time to get down to business. "You might not like me but I'm very good at my job. Bartending is not just about mixing a few cocktails. There's a hell of a lot more to it than that. I've got real passion for the job. You can teach people how to mix drinks and tend bar. You can't teach passion."

Nick nodded. "Now you're talking. It's the same in the music business."

"You know music but you don't know bars the way I do. I can help you. I can run this place for you and do a damn good job."

Nothing. I waited a few seconds. Still nothing.

"You're looking at me as a bartender," I said. "For a

minute, look at me as a bar *manager*, because I can turn this bar around for you."

"I'm refurbishing. That'll bring in more people and turn the bar around."

"You still need a manager. The place isn't going to run itself and you're not going to do it either. In six months, you'll probably be back on the road."

He shook the hair off his face. "Okay, you've got me there. Maybe I should hire a bar manager."

"And it should be me."

"Really?"

"I've worked in lots of bars and I've got plenty of ideas on how to improve the place."

"Such as?"

"The first thing you need to do is fix the bathrooms. The ladies' room is disgusting. If women are too freaked to go to the bathroom, they won't come back. And you need to get women through the door to attract the men."

He didn't look convinced.

"That's one of the basics of the bar business. You've got to start trusting me because I know what I'm talking about."

Still nothing. I'd never seen him this way, had no idea he could be so quiet. Nerves fluttered in my stomach.

"Then there are the Thursday and Friday lunches," I said. "We should have them on the weekends too. That's a no-brainer. If anything, weekends should be even more popular than weekdays. I have no clue why it was only set up for the two days, unless maybe the cook didn't want to work weekends."

"Okay."

"Another thing. The bar is dead quiet in the early

evening so we need to bring people into the bar earlier so we have an early crowd and a late crowd. A happy hour might do the trick, or we could offer free chicken wings or bar snacks. That'll make them thirsty so they have to order more drinks."

Nick nodded for me to continue.

"We could have designated theme nights, all focused around music. Rockabilly is a small but loyal crowd so we could make that a Wednesday or Thursday. We could have dance lessons early and then bring on a band a bit later. Another night of the week, we could have hip-hop or rap. It's not my thing but it'd bring in a bright, young crowd."

"I like the sound of that."

I looked him in the eye because the next bit was going to be a touchy subject. "Some of the staff drink while they're at work and that's got to stop."

"Says who? They don't get drunk, just have a drink or two."

My eyes narrowed. "This is their place of work, not a frat party. I do my best but I can't stop them because I'm not the boss. And also because the boss is drinking."

Nick pushed his chair back, rubbed his chin, and put his feet up on the desk. How could he do that? This was important to me.

Anger flickered in my stomach, then rose to my throat. "Get your feet off the desk."

He flinched, then glared at me.

"Please," I added with as much humility as I could gather.

He took one foot off, then the other. Didn't look impressed.

I straightened in my chair. "If I was to be bar manager,

I'd also need the power to hire and fire staff."

"Hmmm."

"You'd need to believe in me or this will never work. A manager needs lots of tools in his or her arsenal to properly manage a bar."

He stared. "You're a hard ass, Tara. It's what I thought when I first saw you and it's what I think now too."

"That's why I'd be an excellent bar manager."

A moment's silence, then it was as if a light bulb went off in his head. His shoulders relaxed, his whole demeanor changing. I swallowed. This was either going to go extremely well for me, or he'd tell me to get the hell out of here. There'd be no 'in between'. We'd gone too far for that.

"The job's yours," he said.

I grinned. "Really?"

He nodded. "Really."

My heart was racing because there was one more thing we needed to discuss. "There's also the small matter of money."

He laughed, not in a bad way, and we came to an agreement about the money side of things, an arrangement that made me very happy because the extra money would make life a lot easier for me and Eliza.

We shook hands on it, and I had the feeling Nick was starting to act more like an owner.

I still had to ask for an extra day off so I could have a long weekend in New York with Austin. I'd given Nick enough of a shock today so I'd save that for another time. I reached down to pick up my purse from the foot of the chair, ready to leave.

Nick got up opened the office door for me. "So what's

going on with you and Austin?"

That was a bit freaky, almost as if he'd been reading my mind. "Did Austin say anything?"

"It's what he *didn't* say."

I stood. "We're seeing each other."

He raised his eyebrows. "You and Austin."

"Yep, that's right."

"So why didn't he just tell me outright?"

I could ask a similar question—why didn't Austin tell me he was leaving the band? There was no point going there and I still felt a pang when I thought about it. But this was different.

"Because I asked him not to mention it," I said.

"How come?"

"I wanted to get the bar manager job on my own merits."

Nick laughed, let out a whoop.

"What's so funny?" I asked.

"Oh, don't worry. The reason you got this job has nothing to do with Austin and everything to do with the way you laid it on the line. Most people suck up to me because I play in a band and they think I'm famous. Not you. You're as tough as nails. Tougher."

I wasn't sure how to take this. "That's ... good."

He waved it off. "That stuff about only wanting to get the job on your own merits is a load of crap. Other people lie and cheat and shaft their friends to get what they want. It wouldn't have been out of line for you to use your connections. People do it all the time."

He was telling me I didn't need to do everything on my own. But I did.

"By the way." I stopped by the door. "Thanks."

And I left.

CHAPTER THIRTEEN

Austin

Just my luck I'd found the only woman who didn't believe in cabs. Instead, Tara believed in taking the subway like a local and seemed to know the subway system inside out. Even though we'd eaten at a restaurant near the Prince Street subway, that line didn't take us anywhere near our hotel in The Village so we were walking instead.

Which didn't suit me at all. After a day wandering the city and a relaxing meal in Soho, I didn't want to be on my feet. I wanted to be in bed. With Tara.

"I'm a rock star," I said, my tongue firmly in my cheek. "I'm not supposed to walk. Forget the cab. I should've ordered a limo."

Tara nudged me as we ambled up the street. "Why not a helicopter?"

"Now there's an idea." A couple of fat drops of rain landed on my face. "I told you they were rain clouds up there."

"No." That was a guilty voice if I'd ever heard one. She walked a little quicker.

The next drop was so huge it landed on the pavement

with a big thunk. Then another. And another. This wasn't looking good. Sure enough, within seconds rain was pelting down on us.

"Let's make a run for it." She grabbed my hand and ran, her head down to keep the rain from her face.

My hair was the first thing to get wet. Tara's too. Spotting a cab, I stepped between the parked cars and waved. Even though it was occupied, I hoped for the best, then watched as it sped by.

I pointed across the road. "Let's get shelter over there."

"No, there's bound to be a cab up on the corner."

I took her hand again and we ran. It seemed the thing to do. I accidentally stepped in a puddle, water soaking right through my black suede creepers and splashing Tara at the same time.

"Hey!" she said.

As if a little more water was going to make any difference. By the time we got to the corner, my jeans were stuck to my thighs like sheets of wet cardboard, my jacket soaked and heavy on my shoulders.

A guy stood in a doorway surrounded by umbrellas, asking if we wanted to buy one but it was a bit late for that. It amazed me how people like him came out of the woodwork at times like this.

I put my arm around Tara. "I thought you said it wasn't going to rain."

"It might stop soon." That guilty voice again.

I laughed, no point crying, and she snickered too.

"This isn't going to let up anytime soon." I signaled for another cab but the streets were relatively quiet and the only cabs around were taken.

Tara's sodden clothes were clinging to her, which wasn't necessarily a bad thing. She'd styled her hair into a fancy style with a big bow in her hair. Had. Past tense. Because it was now hanging in wet ropes around her face.

"The wet-ragdoll-look suits you," I teased.

She gave me a shove.

"Hey, it wasn't my idea to walk."

Stepping ahead, she said over her shoulder, "Then we might as well keep walking."

She had a point. It wasn't as though we could get any wetter when we were both already soaked right through. It sure as hell increased our walking pace and made us move as fast as humanly possible without running.

I'd only been through Washington Square Park in the day and had never seen it like this. The fountain was lit up, the arch too, but there was hardly anyone around to admire it except for two groups of young people who, like us, were soaked through.

"You seem to know the neighborhood well," I said.

Tara shrugged. "Not really. I lived in a tiny apartment in Queens and I wasn't there for very long anyway."

As soon as we walked in the front door of our hotel, the concierge asked if there was anything he could get us. We just laughed.

The first thing I did when we walked into our room was pull the drapes shut. During the day, I'd enjoyed the view across to the other brownstones and the street below but tonight there was no need for anyone else to see in.

I turned to see Tara shivering, her arms wrapped around herself.

"You should have a shower," I said. "To warm up."

"Okay."

I joined her in the bathroom. She peeled off her wet cardigan, then fumbled with the zipper at the back of her dress, and turned her back to me.

"Can you help?" she asked.

I pulled down the zipper to reveal the creamy skin on her back, then unclasped her bra, and watched as she peeled off her panties. This was no hardship on my part at all. Anytime she needed help taking her clothes off, I could be there for her.

In seconds, she was behind the glass in shower recess. I couldn't keep my eyes off her. Couldn't get my clothes off quickly enough either.

The bathroom had two showers, one for him and one for her. Screw that for a joke. I stepped under the warm spray beside Tara.

She shrieked. "You're cold."

"Not for long."

I ran my hands over her hips, her waist, her boobs. Every bit of her was soft and womanly and everything I'd ever wanted. She snaked her hands around my neck and looked up at me through wet lashes, then pulled my head down and kissed me hard.

Her hands wandered too, over my butt, my hips, till she had her little hands wrapped around me. Heaven was close, so close.

She leaned back against the tiled wall, her lips parted as she pulled me closer. This wasn't slow and loving. It was hard and fast, no holding back as she came in seconds and I followed suit.

Afterward, we were both still panting as the warm spray of water washed over us. Sated. For now. And tired too. It had been a long day of wandering around downtown, then some shopping in midtown and queuing for the Empire State Building. I'd teased her that she'd have to get another tattoo.

As Tara was drying herself, I flicked my towel at her, made her laugh. Such a beautiful sound. I passed her one of the white bathrobes, finished drying myself, and joined her on the leather sofa in the living area.

She had her legs tucked under herself and looked like a ball of fluffy softness, her long dark hair falling over her shoulders. Her hands on the lapels of my bathrobe, she pulled me close and kissed me.

"Is it too early for bed?" I nuzzled closer. "We don't have to sleep right away."

"I'll wait a bit. My hair's still wet."

"You look good wet."

She gave me a playful slap.

And I knew. This was what I wanted. Tara had come onto the scene with a bang but that initial impact had worn off and somehow after that she'd crept up on me, her presence permeating my life and giving it substance.

I didn't just know it. I felt it in every breath I took.

"Why don't you move in with me? You and Eliza, that is."

Tara's lips parted, her eyes wide. "Where did that come from?"

I took her hand and placed it over my heart. "From here."

She kept looking at me. Didn't say anything.

I was so certain this was right. Part of me must have known when I'd been talking to my father the other day too. I'd told him all about Tara, how she'd done it hard and it had made her strong, how she was tough and soft and beautiful.

"Is everything all right?" I asked.

"Sure, I just … I need to think about it, that's all."

"I know it's a bit of a shock for you." It was a shock for me too, a wonderful one, but I didn't tell her that. "And you've got Eliza to think about too."

"Yes, Eliza, that's it." She didn't sound sure of herself.

"What is it, Tara? What else?"

She looked up at me with those pale eyes rimmed with dark lashes. Her skin was so pale, so smooth, positively glowing. Suddenly she looked young, too young to have so much on her shoulders.

"The last time I lived with a guy, it didn't turn out so well," she said.

"How's that?"

"I was in upstate New York and then Mom overdosed—the first time, that is—and I knew I had to come to Frankston to look after Eliza. Turns out that Daniel, the guy I was living with, my so-called boyfriend, didn't care very much. About me or the fact my mom had overdosed."

"Or about Eliza, I take it?"

"She definitely didn't come into it. After a year together, he said it was probably for the best and that we'd had a good run. That was it. Adios amigos."

I twisted my mouth. "Bet that didn't go down well."

"I screamed and shouted at him. Didn't want to let him get off easy. Didn't let him see me cry either because I couldn't bear for him to know how much it had hurt. He didn't care. Not one little bit. And that hurt."

I took her hand into mine. "I'm not like that, Tara. I care about you very much. I'd never leave you in the lurch.

Anyway, he was just one man."

She sighed. "No, just the most recent. I also lived with a guy when I first moved to New York into my crappy apartment in Queens. That didn't work out. Didn't last very long either, only a few months, and then I found the city was too expensive so I had to move again, this time to another town with a friend. I was young then, still in my teens."

"You moved around a lot."

"Yep. A lot more than I would have liked. My mom shifted to a new town every couple of years, dragged us with her. I don't want to be like that."

"I'm not asking you to move to another town."

She pulled her hand back, wrapped her arms around herself. "I know. I have to think about what's best for Eliza too. She needs stability, needs to know she can rely on me, and maybe I need some security too."

Perhaps I was looking for the same thing myself. I was going through a hell of lot of changes with leaving the band, moving back to Frankston, and getting back into architecture. Going from playing in a huge rock band to having a regular job was a quantum leap and sure as hell hadn't been an easy decision to make.

But with Tara, I didn't need to deliberate.

"Look," I said. "There's plenty of space at my place and I need someone to help make it a home because it's pretty barren at the moment."

"It is kind of empty."

"Eliza can have her own room. She can practically have her own entertaining zone, and there's a big kitchen and living area."

Tara's place was falling apart but I didn't want to make

her feel bad about that or point out the obvious. Better to point out the benefits of living with me.

"Grandma's place is still our home," she said. "We're lucky to have it."

"You'll still have it. You don't have to sell the place. It's just that you won't be living there." I pulled her close, let her lean her head against me, pressed a kiss to her damp hair. "Why don't you sleep on it and see how you feel in the morning? Take all the time you need. I'm not going anywhere."

At least we'd have another couple of days, time together with no interruptions, and no one to bother us.

I'd been dead keen to get away from Frankston and have a few days to myself—to ourselves—but it hadn't changed anything. I'd have to go back to the same Frankston and deal with the guys from the band and my father and my change in career.

And Tara. The one thing I didn't want to change.

CHAPTER FOURTEEN

Tara

Talk about coming back down to earth with a crash. When my phone had rung while I was still lying in bed in the hotel room, I'd still been half asleep and it hadn't quite registered. Then the sound of Eliza's voice at the other end, her quiet "hello" had sent a bolt of panic shooting through me.

Even in my muddled state, I'd done the math in my head. If it was seven in New York, it was four in the morning in Frankston and that could only be bad news. What on earth was she doing up at that time?

Partying, as it happened. A party that had gotten out of hand.

We'd taken the first plane back. Austin had been on the phone right away, booking flights, working out the quickest way, not a word of complaint. He'd been wonderful, reliable, everything I could possibly want.

And at the same time, I knew this was all wrong.

Here I was, home again. Eliza flew out of the front door to greet us as soon as the cab pulled up outside the house, offering to take my bag for me. Yep, she was on her best behavior.

I stood on the front porch. "What happened to the window?"

It had taken us all day to get here because the direct flights had all been booked out, so now it was dark out, the front light on. Eliza had told me the window had been smashed—one of many things that had been broken—but it clearly wasn't shattered anymore.

"I had it fixed," she said. "I couldn't leave it broken all day. Anyone could come in or break in with the window like that."

I didn't point out that technically they wouldn't need to break in. "Who fixed it for you?"

"I found someone on the internet who worked on weekends."

Which would have cost a fortune. "How did you pay for it?"

"Out of my savings." She must've seen the look on my face because she added, "I'll pay for everything, Tara, I promise."

Austin placed his hand on my lower back. "Let's go inside."

I let Eliza take my bag while I stomped into the living room to find the drapes ripped, no doubt the result of the same incident that had led to the broken window. Eliza had already given me the stupid story about two boys fighting over a phone.

My sister had done a stellar job cleaning up, that much was clear, but there wasn't much she could do about the dents in the doorframe and the red wine stain on the rug. I didn't think teenagers even drank red wine. Then I noticed the space in the corner of the room, my heart sinking instantly.

"Where's Grandma's chair?"

"I'm sorry, Tara. It's in pieces on the back porch."

"Damn it, Eliza!" Shouting now, I couldn't help myself. "Of all the things in the house, it had to be Grandma's chair. What the hell were you thinking?"

My chest heaving, I was on the verge of losing my shit even more than I already had earlier. I didn't need to tell her that wasn't just a chair. It was as if a piece of Grandma had been ripped from the room. How many times had I sat in that chair relaxing with a cup of tea and it would be almost as if I could feel her in the room?

Austin sidled up closer and said in a low voice, "I'll take a look later on. I might be able to fix it."

A kind offer but there was so much that was beyond repair. I swallowed the anger at the back of my throat because I was fuming at my sister. And at myself for letting this happen.

I should have been here. At the very least I should have seen this coming. I didn't have a relative to bundle her off to for the weekend while I went away, which meant I should never have gone. I'd let her down.

Guilt etched into Eliza's features, I could see she was filled with remorse and was trying her best to make up for what she'd done. And I felt for her, truly I did, because she was young and there was so much she didn't know. I also wanted to kill her. So many conflicting emotions bubbling up inside me.

"Wait here," I said. "I'll put my bag away and be right back."

Also, I was feeling a bit delicate and wanted to check my room was still in one piece. Depositing my bag in the corner of the room, I switched on the light and walked around to make sure everything was as I'd left it. At the far end of the room, I was admiring the freshly vacuumed rug when I saw something under the edge of the bed. A rubber.

Fuming, I marched back into the living room where Eliza and Austin were still standing around, both of them looking uncomfortable.

I put my hands on my hips. "Eliza, why is there a used condom on the floor in my room?"

Horror on her face. "I must've missed it."

Austin covered his mouth, trying to hold back a smirk. I glared at him.

"It wasn't me!" Eliza said. "By the time I found them in there it was too late."

"Having sex in my bedroom?"

"I'm sorry. I washed the sheets and comforter and made your bed. I sugar soaped the nightstand and anything they might've touched. Did everything I could."

I didn't look at Austin. Didn't want him to tell me it wouldn't be the first time someone had had sex in my room.

I pressed my fingers to my temples to hold back a headache that was building. We couldn't stand around all evening so I dropped down onto the sofa, Austin beside me. Eliza sat down gingerly on one of the club chairs. Perched on the edge, her hands clasped in front of her, she reminded me of a nun.

Shouting at her wasn't doing either of us any good. I had to be mature and in control of the situation because she sure as hell wasn't. Besides, shouting was what our mother used to do and I didn't want to be like her.

"I don't get it, Eliza. We were away on Saturday night and that was fine. Then, on Sunday night, you had a huge party. Why? Especially when you guys all had to go to school today. I mean, you're always so focused on your studies. It doesn't make sense."

She looked down. "I wanted to have the party on Saturday but Michaela had a wedding that day, her cousin's, so Saturday night was out."

I gritted my teeth. "Michaela…"

"I'm not saying it was her fault." Her lower lip trembled. "It was mine. My decision, a bad one. Just because she suggested it didn't mean I had to go along with the idea. I don't know what I was thinking."

"Yeah, well, neither do I."

"Michaela was terrible about the whole thing." Tears glimmered in my sister's eyes as she lifted her gaze. "She thought this was great fun, a hoot, didn't know why I was getting so worked up when things started going wrong. When I freaked out about the window being broken, she wanted to know what the big deal was. She didn't care. Not one bit."

I sucked in a deep breath. This was exactly what I'd been trying to tell Eliza all along, even if I'd always known she'd work it out on her own eventually. I just hadn't thought it would involve the trashing of our house.

God knows, I'd done enough dumb things when I was young and I'd had plenty of selfish friends too, girls who'd leave me in the middle of nowhere to go off to have sex with some guy, one who stuffed her dope into my purse so she wouldn't get busted. Eventually, I'd worked out they weren't friends.

Eliza was only human too.

"So who did the cleaning up?" I asked.

"Me."

"On your own?"

"Everyone else was at school or maybe in bed, I don't know. I only know they weren't here. Sorry I didn't go to school today. I cleaned up as best I could."

"I hope you've learned from this."

I hated saying that, hated feeling like a parent, but that was what I had to be. I'd already made enough mistakes and had to make up for them too.

Austin cleared his throat. "Eliza, your sister is right. I might be able to put your grandmother's chair back together and I'm planning on fixing the kitchen faucet, but this isn't just about fixing stuff. It's about respect and responsibility."

"I know."

"Not many people would do what Tara is doing for you. She doesn't normally go off enjoying herself and the one time she does, look what happens. She works hard to look after you. Can you see how this comes across, how ungrateful it seems?"

Tears slid down my sister's cheeks. "You're right. Tara, you've been wonderful to me. What I did was so wrong and stupid and I'm lucky it wasn't a lot worse. I still can't get over Michaela." She shook her head. "She even thought it was funny that the police turned up."

Had I heard right? "What?"

I jumped to my feet, then sat back down after Austin put his hand on my arm to reassure me.

Eliza twisted her hands. "Some of the boys had an argument as they were leaving, then started a fight so the neighbors called the police. I was lucky. This was all happening further down the street, then the cops got called away for a shooting or something, and didn't come into the house. I know how bad it would've been if they had, what with all the underage drinking."

"And you?"

Eliza brushed the tears away. "I had a couple of drinks, then sobered up pretty quickly when things started going downhill. Michaela kept drinking. She had a great time. I tried to get everyone to leave but no one was paying any attention to me. I didn't know what to do."

I'd bet my bottom dollar that if it wasn't for Michaela, none of this would have happened. Still, Eliza was right. This had been her decision.

Like leaving my little sister alone and going away for a romantic weekend had been mine. How could I ever have thought that that fairytale might work out?

Austin and I were from two different worlds. He was successful and famous and would no doubt be an excellent architect too, whereas my life was a mess and didn't mesh with his. I worked in a bar, for fuck's sake. If it wasn't for Grandma leaving us the house, Eliza and I would probably be living in a trailer. We were white trash while he was rock royalty.

I'd been fooling myself. Part of me had always known things would fall apart with Austin sooner or later. It wasn't meant to be. The happy-ever-after didn't work for girls like me, not because I didn't deserve it but because that's the way things were. Instead, despair gripped my heart, cut right through me.

At least I'd done one better than my mother had, and I was trying to set Eliza up for greater success. College if we could afford it and a career where she was respected and could mix with a better crowd. The least I could do was get that bit right.

"I'm sorry, Tara." Eliza sobbed gently, kept talking. "For everything, for the mess I made and Grandma's chair and the window. And I'm sorry you had to leave New York early." She hiccupped a big sob, then pulled herself together. "But I had to call you. I had to. I didn't know what to do. I felt so alone."

I wanted to put my arm around her and tell her it'd all be better. I wanted to do that so badly it was burning a hole in my chest. And if I was just a sister, I would have. I'd have held her in my arms and rocked her the way I had after Mom died.

But now I had to act like a parent. I bit back the tears.

"I'm sorry too, Eliza. I can't let this go. You're grounded for two months. You can go to basketball because I've already paid for your sports, but other than that, it's school then straight home."

Tears streaming down her face, she sniffled. "I understand. That's only fair. It's a long time but I deserve it."

Austin reached across to squeeze my hand. It should have been reassuring. He was a good man doing all the right things.

And it wasn't enough.

I'd made a big mistake. I'd fallen for him. When I was with him, I didn't think about anything else. Or anyone. And that was the problem because I should be thinking about Eliza, at least for the next few years.

I didn't blame her. Deep down, I'd always known this wasn't going to work.

CHAPTER FIFTEEN

Austin

Looking around the studio, I knew I'd made the right decision. With its polished concrete floor and large windows letting in natural light, the place could have been something from an architecture magazine except it didn't look minimal, not with the drawing boards, Macs, and clutter on the desks. This was a working office, no doubt about it.

Matthew, one of the architects, shook my hand as soon as I walked through the door and led me through the studio. "Your dad has told us so much about you. I'm looking forward to working with you. I'm a big fan too, by the way."

It wasn't his words so much as the excitement in his voice and the grin he couldn't get off his face that told me he was beside himself at meeting me. I got this all the time and couldn't wait to be just a regular guy.

"Thanks, I can't wait to get back into architecture." I pointed to the glass wall behind which Dad was sitting in his office. "It's in my blood."

He laughed way too loudly. "Oh, sure. Like father, like

son. Go straight in."

Dad looked up from his desk. "Close the door behind you."

I did so, then stayed looking out across the office. "Matthew seems rather young."

"No, he's thirty-six. He's just a little start struck, that's all."

I turned to face my father and sat down. "Yeah, I get that sometimes. It won't take long for the novelty to wear off."

"Exactly what I was thinking." He pushed some papers away, leaned back in his chair. "You're one of the team now. Or you will be soon. I wanted you to look around so you knew what you might be missing."

"Missing?"

"Yes, I asked you here for a reason."

I still wasn't sure what that was. "Look, there's something I wanted to tell you too." I was smiling before I'd even said her name. "I asked Tara to move in with me."

Silence. Dad's face was immobile. He was never one to give much away.

"You're moving mighty fast, son."

I had a bad feeling about where this was headed. "I guarantee you I've met women who move a hell of a lot faster than she does. I asked *her*, not the other way around, and I know what I want."

"On the contrary, maybe there are a few things you should know about that girl."

"Woman." I jumped in quickly, didn't like the tone of my father's voice. "Her sister is a girl. She's sixteen. Tara is a woman."

He pursed his lips. "I asked around about her."

"What for?"

"You know what Frankston is like. If you move in the right circles, someone always knows someone else."

I gritted my teeth. "You didn't answer my question."

"Her mother was a drug addict and a stripper. I bet Tara didn't tell you that."

I hadn't heard the bit about her being a stripper before but couldn't say it surprised me.

"I don't really care what her mother did for a living. It doesn't reflect on Tara."

He scoffed. "You know what strippers are like. I'm not going to mince my words. They give hand jobs under the table and do god-only-knows what else. It's one step up from a prostitute. Hell, she may have been one of those too for all I know. My point is, Tara's not from a good family, certainly not good enough for you."

My pulse rate rose instantly, my heart racing, anger building. Good old Dad was getting straight to the point. No beating around the bush.

"Since most of Tara's family is dead," I said, "I don't particularly care what they used to do for a living. Tara works hard and she's just got a promotion."

"She's a barmaid, for crying out loud!"

"And her sister is an excellent student. Tara has made great sacrifices to do the best for her and look after her. Not many people would do what she's doing."

No need to mention the party Eliza had while we were away or Dad would twist it into something worse than it was and make out like she was a delinquent. Anyone could make a mistake and Eliza was young.

Besides, something had happened with Tara since the

party and she wasn't quite herself. Quieter, calmer, it wasn't like her.

I stared at my father. "When did you get to be so judgmental?"

A dumb question. He'd always had a superior attitude.

Dad stared right back at me as if I was an idiot. "You can't possibly be serious about her? She's good for a bit of fun, sure, but nothing more than that."

A bit of fun. My blood boiling, I clenched my fists to stop myself from shouting and screaming. The man had no idea, no clue at all.

He wanted an architect son who'd marry the right sort of person, mix in superior circles, and lead an acceptable upper middle class life. He'd never understood my love for music, rockabilly, the band. He'd always thought it a passing phase. He didn't know me at all.

And he'd already made his mind up about Tara.

I straightened in my chair. "I didn't come back home so you could tell me what to do and how to live my life."

"No, you came back here to return to architecture. You can't do that without me."

"Pardon?"

I didn't know how I could be so polite when I was about to boil over. Maybe it hadn't sunk in, but it was starting to. Did my father really think there was no way to do this without him? Did he think so little of me?

Dad's eyes narrowed. "You need me."

With those three small words, he said everything. It was such a cliché. *You need me.*

Selfish? Self-opinionated? Yes, I'd always known he was those things. But an asshole? The one thing I'd never thought of him. Until now.

My chest swelled to bursting, anger surging, fury ready to spew forth. I wanted to pick the chair up and smash it against the wall.

No, I wasn't going to lose it in a glass-fronted office for everyone to see. I wouldn't give him the satisfaction. Dad waited, wanting to see my reaction. That was the way he worked.

I took a deep breath, forced myself to slow down. "I need a lot of things. I've got plenty of money but I still need a job. I *want* a job." My voice caught in my throat. "Do I need a father? You tell me."

Dad looked down his nose at me. "Do you think anyone else will take you on after I put the word out?"

He had to be kidding. "What word?"

"Architecture is a small industry. It doesn't take long for word to get around. What will people think if they find out I refused to have my own son at my practice because he doesn't have the necessary skills and experience?"

I took to my feet. "Do I look like I care?"

Damn it, Dad was the only one not losing his cool and I couldn't bear for him to get the better of me.

He reclined back in his chair. "You've got no future with that girl. She's no good and you know it. You want the girl and you want the job. Well, you can't have both. It's her or a position at the practice."

My jaw clenched, I forced myself to speak. "You've never been like this before. Not this bad anyway. What's gotten over you?"

He stood, leaned over his desk, pointed through the window. "See all those people out there, they work for me on my terms. I'm the boss. I oversee every design. Everything that goes out of here has my name on it and I stand by my architecture firm."

I shook my head. "This isn't about the job. I don't know what the hell is going on with you and I don't care. You can take your job and shove it. This is about something more important. My self respect."

And my future and a wonderful woman and a lot of other things I wasn't going to get into right now because I couldn't stand being in that office a minute longer. He was wasting my time when I should be thinking of Tara, spending more time together, celebrating the good things in life.

At least I had one job, The Swamp renovation. And one was more than none.

I pulled open the door and turned to see him standing with his fist raised.

"You'll come running back with your tail between your legs."

Another cliché. I'd wanted to work for my dad and to return to architecture. But not like this.

CHAPTER SIXTEEN

Tara

Austin had something on his mind, I could tell. Then again, so did I.

He popped open the champagne. "We should celebrate."

I didn't feel like champagne at a time like this but there was nothing I could do to stop him. We were sitting on the stools at his kitchen counter because he didn't have any living room furniture and we needed a table of sorts. The stools probably cost as much as all of my lounge and dining furniture put together. He might not have a lot of furniture but he sure didn't skimp.

"You look a bit down," he said. "You're not still mad at Eliza."

"Well, yes, but she's been fantastic this last week. The perfect sister, polite and cleaning up after herself."

"Her heart's in the right place even if she did screw up."

I nodded. "Yeah, I can see she's not just going through the motions. She's genuine, trying to show me she cares."

He poured the Veuve. "Of course she cares. She's got

a wonderful sister and she knows it."

"Thanks."

Austin was being kind and meanwhile, I was thinking about breaking up with him. It only made me feel worse, nerves simmering in my stomach. I swallowed back the guilt.

I'd come to his place so that when the time came, after I'd had my say, I could leave. Because, otherwise, I wouldn't have the strength to go through with this.

He picked up the two glasses, handed me one. "Congratulations to the new bar manager. I hope you knock 'em dead at The Swamp."

I smiled wanly as I took a sip. "Thanks."

The bubbles should have made me more relaxed but they disagreed with me. I couldn't drink. I couldn't do this. My heart sank even more but I forced myself to go through with it.

"I've been thinking about things," I began.

He nodded. "I've been giving the bar a lot of thought too. I don't need my father or his firm to renovate the premises. I'm not joining his practice after all. I've spoken to Ryan, an old friend from architecture, who has one or two small clients of his own, and we're joining forces, starting up our own practice."

This was news to me. "Really?"

"Yep." A muscle in his jaw flinched, which seemed odd for a guy who seemed so certain. "It'll definitely be a good thing in the long run."

I steeled myself. "It's kind of the long-term that I've been thinking of too."

"Yeah, I've been wondering about the bar. Do you think Nick really wants to be a bar owner?"

"I'm not sure." It was easier to think about Nick than other things. "When he first came to town, I'd have said no, definitely not. At first it seemed like he bought The Swamp on a whim as much as anything and I'm sure he had no idea how much hard work was involved in owning and running a bar."

"And now?"

"He's lifted his game. It took a major kick up the butt and he's listening at least."

Austin grinned. "And who better to kick his butt than you?"

Normally his proud demeanor would have made me smile. Today it sent an uncomfortable shiver up my spine because I didn't deserve his affection and couldn't bear to go there.

"Things have changed for him," Austin said. "When he first came to town, he was looking for a hobby."

"And now?"

"Now he wants nothing more than to get back with Lily and look after his family. They've had some issues, serious ones after Thomas's accident, but they're working on it. Or Nick is, anyway. He's not just after a good time anymore."

I hoped things worked out for Nick. We may have butted heads but he was a decent guy and seemed to be getting his act together.

"That explains a few things," I said. "His change in attitude, for one."

"I need to talk to him some more about the renovations. I might suss him out for something else I had in mind."

"What's that?"

"He might not be so interested in being a bar owner anymore. He might want to sell. If that was the case, we could buy the place together, the two of us."

My chest swelled, then tightened. That was what I'd always wanted and had barely dared to admit even to myself because it was so far out of my reach it wasn't funny.

But it wasn't my fantasy or my goal anymore. That wasn't why I'd come here.

I swallowed. "That's a pipe dream for someone like me. I can barely get by as it is. I don't have that sort of money, nowhere near it."

"I do."

He let his words settle. Still, this was all wrong.

"Think about it, Tara." His voice was soft, sultry, imploring. "We'd be partners. I'd provide the collateral and architectural expertise for the renovations, and you'd be running the place. You're the one with bar experience and more business acumen than you realize. I couldn't do it without you. Wouldn't even think about it without you."

Elbows on the counter, I pressed my fingers to my temples to try to stop my head from swirling.

Austin lowered his voice. "Think about it, that's all I'm saying. It's just an idea. It might not come off. Nick might not want to sell but if he does we should be ready to leap."

That was the whole problem. I'd leapt into love with Austin, let myself fall for him, and he'd made me feel secure in his arms. I'd wanted some stability and had wallowed in it, wanted it to be more than it was, yearned for more than I could get. Reckless. Stupid. Because this would've been a hell of a lot easier if I didn't love him.

And now my heart was being pulled in two directions.

"Think about Eliza too," he added. "While you're bar manager, The Swamp will start pulling off the big bucks and you'll still be earning the same wage whereas as the owner, you'd be reaping the profits. Eliza would be better off in the long run too."

He was talking about the long-term. He wanted me to be part of his life. Was that what he was saying? Longing clawed away inside me because I wanted so badly for this to be true.

He got along so well with Eliza and supported me in my role in every way. Maybe this would be the right thing for her too and we could do this after all. And for me, most of all for me. Maybe I deserved a little love in my life too.

"I-I'm not sure," I stuttered.

"There'd be contracts and lawyers of course."

"Of course," I said, though I hadn't given that a second thought.

"It'll be the perfect business arrangement so that if one of us pulls out, the demarcation is clear and we each know exactly where we stand."

My heart clenched. "A business arrangement…"

"Not that I think you'd pull out, but we need to have all the bases covered."

"Who said I'd be pulling out?"

"That's not what I meant. This is business. You have to be prepared for every eventuality. It's the standard way things are done, otherwise people end up with a mess they can't handle."

This wasn't what I wanted to hear. Tears burned at the back of my eyes but I clenched my jaw and held them at bay. I wouldn't cry, wouldn't let him know how much this hurt. I was a business arrangement, an eventuality, a contract to be prepared and signed so that we were both ready when our time came to an end. He was planning for our demise.

I wanted him all or nothing, and I'd been fooling myself that I could have it all when I should have known better. I'd had the right idea in the first place.

He reached for my hand. I pulled it back. Didn't want him to feel how I was shaking.

Austin held my gaze. "Tara…"

I cleared my throat to keep the quaver from my voice. "Something about this doesn't sit right with me."

"Look, my parents are divorced and I remember how messy it was when they split up. They both ended up feeling like they'd got a raw deal and that's exactly what I want to avoid because I saw how it affected the two of them and Dad's architecture practice. Much better to have things clear from the start."

I slid off the stool, steadied myself on the counter. "My folks never bothered getting married. Dad disappeared. Mom got by on booze and pills. It doesn't mean I'm going to go through the same things. I learned a lot from them too. I learned what *not* to do, how not to live my life, and I'm not going to make those same mistakes."

He stood from the stool, his eyes filled with fear and uncertainty. The frown on his face told me he couldn't see I might want more, much more than he could give me.

I lowered my gaze. It was too dangerous to keep looking at him when he was everything that I wanted and all that I couldn't have. My legs were weakening beneath me but I couldn't let this dilute my resolve.

"Tara." His voice was low. "If buying the bar is too much for you, we can trash the idea. That's all it was, an idea. It doesn't have to come between us."

The problem was that it told me so much about him. I was never going to be a long-term proposition and he was planning for our break-up. So was I. Sooner than him.

I lifted my gaze. "I'm not the right girl for you, Austin."

"Says who?"

"I can't move in with you. I have to do what's best for me and Eliza. I'm sorry, more sorry than you can know. But it doesn't change the fact it's over."

"Over?" Shock in his eyes. He hadn't seen this coming.

He grabbed my arm. "You're more important to me than the bar or a stupid contract."

My lips pursed together, I shook my head. My eyes were already filling with tears and I had to get the hell out of there before they started falling or, worse, I changed my mind.

I pulled my arm out of his grasp, turned, and marched out the door. I had to look after my family, and Eliza was all I had left. Austin was never going to be my family. Family was forever.

And he wasn't.

CHAPTER SEVENTEEN

Austin

I'd tried calling Tara but there wasn't much I could do if she didn't want to speak to me. I'd screwed up, made the biggest mistake of my life. Everything I'd said had come out all wrong and everything Tara had said was true.

I could blame my current situation on my father for being a hard-nosed businessman, for failing in his relationship with Mom, for setting a bad example for me.

Or I could blame myself.

Still, I had to finish what I'd started so it'd been good timing when Eliza had gotten in touch. She had an early finish on Thursdays and was home by lunchtime. That was the story she gave me, anyway, and she was so diligent I didn't think she'd cut class. Meanwhile, Tara was working the busy lunch shift, otherwise I wouldn't have dreamed of coming over, but I did want to fix up a couple of things at the house. I'd promised.

Besides, when I was talking to Eliza it felt like there was a small piece of Tara here and maybe a sliver of hope. The two of us were on the back patio and it was getting warm even in the shade.

She kneeled down beside me to peer at the chair I was repairing. "Wow, you're really good at this."

"Practice." I'd had a lot of it.

"But how do you know this stuff?"

"I've always been interested in how things are put together and that makes it easier to work out how to put them back the way they were."

A pause. "I really appreciate it."

It turned out Grandma's chair wasn't as bad as it looked. It had fallen to pieces but each of the pieces was basically still intact so it was a matter of reassembling the chair, tightening the joints, and making sure it was all square.

"I'm glad I called you." She let out a huge sigh of relief, overdid it. "It's not just the chair. It's so good having human contact."

"You go to school, don't you?" I looked across at her. "There are other humans there too, aren't there?"

She twisted her mouth. "It's not the same. I can't go out, can't have friends over." A change in her tone. "I'm not complaining. This punishment thing is fair enough and, I mean, punishment isn't supposed to be fun. I get it."

"Yep, glad you've got the hang of that."

She shrugged. "It hasn't been that bad, I guess. Loads of kids have been coming up and talking to me, saying how they feel for me. Kids who wouldn't normally talk to me. Some cute guys too."

"Cute guys?"

"Well, yeah."

"And Michaela?"

Her eyes narrowed. "Michaela who? I couldn't care

less about that girl."

"I take it you're not friends anymore."

"I still talk to her, kind of, but we're not exactly friends, which is fine by me because I don't need friends like her."

"And you've got the cute guys now."

She nodded emphatically. "Exactly."

I stood, admired my handiwork. "You'll have to leave the chair for twenty-four hours. Don't touch it. Definitely don't sit on it. And then it'll be as right as rain."

I'd used good old Elmer's glue, my favorite, and had clamped a section of the legs together so it'd hold while the glue was drying. I might have to come back to pick up the clamps. Could be a good excuse to come by.

Eliza pulled down her skirt, struggling a little so I took her hand and helped her up.

"That looks fab." Her eyes were wide. "Thanks so much."

"I'll get going now."

She dragged me back inside. "Not yet. We just have to test the faucet again."

I laughed. "Sure."

Had I ever been that young and enthusiastic? It made me smile. No wonder I liked her so much.

In the kitchen, we turned on the mixer faucet and Eliza insisted I have a glass of water. I didn't mind. Didn't realize how sweaty and thirsty I'd become out on the back patio either.

I'd called in an old buddy who was a qualified plumber to help with the installation because it was too big a job for me. I'd grabbed the faucet, still in its box, from my dad's garage a while ago, which was probably just as well because

I hadn't visited him since we'd had our blow-up.

My gut clenched. He wasn't the man I thought he was. From anyone else I could've brushed it off but from my own father, it cut deep. I forced myself not to think about it. It wasn't as if I didn't have plenty of other things to think about.

I tried to focus on the positives instead—on my budding new architecture business with Ryan, which was the one thing I had going for me at the moment.

He was thrilled that our first commission would be The Swamp because it'd be an excellent crossover between the bar business and the creative side of things. He'd scored a job too, a new café being set up by a young baker and a barista, so between us we had enough to get the ball rolling.

All in all, it looked like I had myself a partner. It was a good move, great actually, but it was hard to be outwardly excited about it when I'd lost something that was much more important than money or a career.

Tara. A huge loss. I couldn't shake the dread that filled my stomach, the weight I carried around with me, the pain that wouldn't go away.

I heard the click of keys in the front door from the other end of the house. That must be her. Longing simmered deep inside me. I didn't know if this would be good or bad and wasn't sure how this would go.

"I should get going," I said.

Eliza raised her eyebrows, a guilty expression on her face. "Why?" Then, more loudly, "Tara, Austin's here."

She was composed by the time she walked into the kitchen. Composed didn't mean happy. And neither was I when I laid eyes on her. Seeing her again when I couldn't have her was a stab in my heart. I stayed cool, didn't let it show.

"I was just leaving," I said. "Eliza called me."

Meanwhile, Eliza was as far as cool as you could get. "Look! It's a mixer. See how easy this is. Flick, flick." She did a demonstration, wasted some more water.

Tara shifted her gaze to me. "Did you do this for us?"

"It's no problem. I said I'd take care of it."

"How much do I owe you?"

"Nothing." I explained why. "I thought you'd be pleased."

She nodded. "Oh, I am. Thank you."

"And he fixed Grandma's chair too," Eliza chimed in.

Tara raised her eyebrows. "Really?"

"Go and take a look. It's on the back patio, but you can't touch it or sit on it yet."

Placing her purse on the countertop, Tara wandered over to the back door and stepped outside.

Eliza turned to me. "You two dumb asses need to talk."

She took me by surprise, nearly knocked me back with her words. It was almost as if an alien had taken over her body, yet at the same time this was the Eliza I knew.

I sucked in some air through my teeth. "Your sister would have your head on a platter if you spoke that way to her."

"Well, duh, I'm not saying it to her. I'm hoping one of you will see sense."

Tara walked back through the door. "Thank you, Austin. I-I don't know what to say."

It took my breath away. *Say you'll have me. Say you don't want me to go.*

"Isn't this wonderful?" Eliza said. "Austin is so clever, so good at fixing stuff."

"And you're so good at breaking things," Tara said, deadpan.

I held her gaze. "You know you can call me ... if there's anything else you need."

She nodded. "Sure."

"I should get going."

Tara saw me to the door, didn't say anything. We brushed arms as she reached for the doorknob and I wondered if she could feel the same sense of loss. Despite the calm demeanor, I was certain something was glimmering in her eyes, reluctance, regret, longing for what could have been. There had to be something there.

I stopped outside the door. The Thunderbird was parked on the street. I loved that car like it was a piece of myself, but now I had a new love in my life, a love that'd been lost, so what was the point?

"I'll see you at the bar," I said. "The renovations won't happen overnight. It's an ongoing process."

"I'll be there."

Was Tara's voice quavering or was that my imagination? I opened my mouth to speak but wasn't sure where to start because what I had to say had everything to do with her and nothing to do with the bar. Should I start at the beginning? The end?

I was only halfway down the front path when I turned back but she'd already disappeared behind the closed door. Regret burned deep inside me.

Tara was right. I'd assumed we wouldn't last so then I'd made sure we didn't. It made me angry. At myself. I didn't have to be like my father. I could be the man I wanted to be.

    And I wasn't done yet.

CHAPTER EIGHTEEN

Tara

Great, Nick thought I was a hard ass. Meanwhile, the sight of Austin strolling into the bar was making my stomach flutter in a not-so-good way and he wasn't even doing anything other than walking. I was going to have to do better than this. I straightened, pulled myself together.

Nick motioned for me to come out from behind the bar and join him. "Come over and meet the new guy, Ryan."

Austin had mentioned this particular friend of his, and I now suspected it must've been a big move for Austin to decide against joining his dad's firm, not that this was any of my business anymore. In fact, it had never been.

I shook hands with a tall skinny guy about Austin's age. "Nice to meet you."

Ryan nodded. "It'll be great to talk to you, get your input. You work here so you know the place pretty well." He looked around. "But this is Austin's baby. I'm only here to look around and offer a second opinion."

"Ryan's modest," Austin said. "He's a very good architect. Won an award last year for an apartment building he designed here in Frankston."

Leaving the band and going back to architecture where he was starting almost from scratch was such a huge step for Austin. I hoped things went well for him, truly I did. I could open my heart up to him at least that much.

"Technically, my boss won the award but that's the way these things work." Ryan turned to Austin. "From now on, any awards will be *ours*."

Austin nodded, looked as if he liked the sound of that. He went through some of his ideas about the layout and flow of the bar with Ryan, making sure to include both me and Nick in the discussion. We wandered to the band room, then came back again, the four of us standing near the door where we had a view across the whole place.

I raised my eyebrows. "You know the layout behind the bar is a mess? I haven't even got into that with Nick."

The short version was that the bar was set up badly, which led to the bartenders having to move around to get ingredients and then tripping over each other. It was bar basics, as far as I was concerned, and I had no clue how the previous owner had let things get this bad.

"I'll take care of you, Tara," Austin said.

My heart stammered in my chest. If only this would work. If only he would take care of me.

"And the other bartenders, of course," he said.

So that was what he'd meant. My stomach dropped but I didn't let it show.

He added, "I'll make sure the bar has at least three or four stations that are properly set up with everything within reach. They'll be your typical Billy The Kid Stations."

"What?" I frowned. "Billy The Kid?"

"That's my name for them. Each bar station should be around four feet wide with the beer taps nearby and the spirits well below with your two soda guns on either side."

He held out his arms as if he had two guns in his hands.

If only I were that tough. Like a gunslinger at a saloon. Someone who rules the Wild West, who others were scared of, who shoots them down before he can get hurt.

I forced a smile to my face. "Yep, like Billy The Kid. That's me."

Austin held my gaze. "I'll make sure the bathrooms are the first things to get renovated."

"Hey," Nick said. "What for?"

"They're disgusting, and you need decent bathrooms for the women. It's turning them off and they're your most important clientele. If you get the females in, the guys will follow. We should do the bathrooms up right away as the first stage of the project, then worry about the other stuff later."

Nick nodded. "Okay."

Okay? I'd been through this with Nick before and he hadn't agreed with me back then even though I'd been trying to coach him through the process.

"Hey!" Frustration sparked in my stomach. "You wouldn't listen when I tried to tell you that."

He spread his arms. "Give me a break. I'm still learning."

And so was I. I was learning that I should never have let myself get involved like this. Then I wouldn't feel this huge sense of loss, and my heart wouldn't have been shattered, the fragments still sharp in my chest. It wouldn't hurt to look at Austin, think about him, and stand here not touching him. It killed me that we were standing so close together when he was so far away.

Austin added, "If we're organized, we might be able to do all the work over three or four days. Pull up the tiles, lay new ones, check the plumbing, install individual urinals in the men's room, new basins, hand dryers, the works."

Plumbing? Was this all that he and I had in common now? My stomach dropped a little further.

Suddenly I didn't care that Nick hadn't listened when I'd told him those things. Didn't care about the bar. Didn't care about any of this. I just wanted to get away. My skin started to crawl. Nerves, fear, I wasn't sure which.

"Austin, I'll leave all that stuff up to you," Nick said. "I trust you. You're the expert."

I had to finish this conversation. "That's decided, then."

Nick looked from me to Austin and screwed up his face. "Why are you two acting so damn professional anyway?"

I bit my lip, didn't want to answer that question, not right now. But I had to say something.

"You're right, Nick," I said. "I should get back to work and leave the experts to it."

Austin got in quickly. "I'll need your input on the bar design. There's more to it than this quick conversation."

I edged back. "When you're ready, then."

"If we're done, I'll get going too," Nick said. "I need to get back to Thomas."

"Everything okay?" Austin asked.

"Yeah, I dropped him off with Lily's mom so I could come here." A huge smile overtook his face. "The little fella will be waiting for me."

I reminded myself Nick was a wonderful father and a good person. I shouldn't take my problems out on him. It wasn't fair.

He was out the door in a flash. Ryan turned to join him, looking over his shoulder at Austin who was still standing there. My heart crumpled, my breath leaving my body. I should be able to deal with this but I couldn't.

Please leave. Please stay.

He reached for my arm, his touch gentle. Meanwhile, the emotions swirling inside me were way out of proportion with the brush of his hand. I pressed my eyes shut, struggling to keep myself together.

"You're good at your job, Tara," he said. "Wonderful with Eliza, good at a lot of things. You've already proven that."

He left. And another piece of my heart left with him.

*　　　*　　　*

One of the other bartenders stuck her head through the door of the staff room where I was taking a break. "There's some guy here to see you."

My heart jumped to my throat. Some guy? No, it didn't necessarily mean it was Austin.

"Some old guy," she added.

"Okay, thanks."

I stood, following her back into the bar to see Austin's father standing there, looking extremely uncomfortable. His father, not Austin. This was turning into one hell of a day.

I stayed on the other side of the bar. "Hi."

"Tara, hello. Can we talk?" He nodded toward the back of the room. "At a table. Do you have a few minutes?"

I hesitated. "Sure."

Something didn't feel right. A lot of things actually, including the fact I had no idea why the man was here.

I wandered out from behind the bar, took my time, tried to get my head together. I'd only met him once before and all I knew about him was what Austin had told me. An architect, divorced, and now Austin wasn't part of his practice anymore.

The two of us had broken up but I didn't know if his father knew that and didn't particularly want to go there. I should've told him I was too busy to talk to him. Too late for that now. I let out a long sigh as I sat at a table at the back of the room.

"It's David, isn't it?" I asked.

"Yes."

"What can I do for you?"

He gave this some consideration. "I made a mistake. Now that's not easy for me to say."

He said this as if anticipating my sympathy, waiting for my response, one I couldn't give because I didn't know what was going on.

I raised my eyebrows. "What mistake was that?"

"I'm sure Austin has told you."

He left it at that, as if I was supposed to do all the talking or read his mind. I had no idea what game he was playing but I was damned if I'd play with him. He could talk or I'd get up and leave. I sat there thin-lipped, staring at the face that resembled Austin's but was so much harder.

One ... two ... I'd give him until five.

Eventually, he said, "I presented him with an ultimatum. A stupid, selfish one. I'm an old man and sometimes things come out all wrong despite my best efforts." He added, "You didn't deserve it and neither did he."

What didn't I deserve? And what did this have to do with me? This rattled me.

David sucked in a deep breath. "Austin won't speak to me, won't take my calls, and didn't answer the door when I visited him. I don't know if he was home at the time or not." He leaned forward, his hands on the table. "Maybe you could talk to him."

I shook my head, tried not to give too much away. Clearly Austin's father didn't know we'd broken up or he wouldn't have come here. Or maybe he did know and something else was going on. Whatever the case, I trusted my gut over this man any day.

"He obviously loves you." He spat the words out.

A pang shot through my chest because I didn't dare think it was true, not for a minute, and not from this man. Somehow I had the feeling he'd eat me up and spit me out if he saw a glimmer of fear.

I steeled myself. "Would that be such a bad thing?"

"You tell me. It's true, isn't it?"

"That's between us."

He spread his arms. "Well, he must be in love with you if he chose you over the architecture practice."

So that was the ultimatum he'd given to Austin. Anger exploded inside me, my breaths coming short and fast.

No, no, don't lose it, Tara, don't let him win. One long slow breath in, one long slow breath out.

I could hear the man's words in my head. I'd heard it all before. I was a lowly barmaid. I was below his son, one step away from trailer trash. The sort of girl you'd fuck but wouldn't marry, not in a hundred years.

Disgust burning at the back of my throat, I gritted my teeth. "You'd better leave right now."

He held a hand out. "Don't be like that. I came here with all the best intentions. I've apologized, said I made a mistake, and now I'm trying to make amends. All I'm asking is for you to suggest to my son that he speak to me. That's not a big call."

I pushed my chair back. "Goodbye, Mr. Murphy."

He leaned across the table, his voice low, his eyes narrow. "I was expecting some screaming and shouting. I thought you had a temper. That's what I'd heard."

My legs were shaking but stood, forcing my voice to stay even. "Not me. You must be thinking about someone else." I pointed to the door where my friend from security was stationed. "Whereas Tyrone over there has a terrible problem with anger management. You wouldn't want to make him mad."

I marched off, glancing back to make sure he'd left, then kept going and didn't stop until I'd made it to the staff room. I closed the door behind me, leaned back against it, and balled my hands into fists to hold back the anger bubbling inside me.

My head was spinning but it all made sense, the pieces falling into place. This was why Austin was starting up a practice with Ryan—because of his father's ultimatum. Austin had seemed edgy on our last night together but hadn't said anything about this. How could he without insulting me?

The sobs came hard and fast, tears streaming down my face. It felt as if my heart had been ripped out and my chest was about to cave in. I couldn't breathe, couldn't get enough air, couldn't work out how it had come to this. I wrapped my arms around myself to hold in the hurt.

What a mess. What a god awful mess.

CHAPTER NINETEEN

Austin

Eliza pulled the front door open. I'd already primed her to let her know I was coming, also to make sure Tara was home. It was a relief to have someone on my side.

"Perfect timing." Eliza couldn't hide the excitement from her voice. "She's in the kitchen. We've had lunch so she won't be all hungry and cranky. I even vacuumed and mopped this morning and did my perfect-sister-impersonation to help get her in a good mood."

I squeezed her hand. "Thanks, Eliza."

She closed the door behind us.

"No problem. Come on through." She marched ahead of me, yelling out at the top of her lungs, "Tara, you've got a visitor!"

In the kitchen, Tara turned from the sink where she was doing the dishes. Her lips were parted, her skin pale and creamy, her dark hair pulled back from her face. No makeup. She didn't need any.

It took my breath away. I felt as if I were looking at her for the first time, almost as if I'd forgotten how beautiful she was, even more alluring than the last time I'd

164

seen her, if that were possible.

"I hope I'm not disturbing you," I said.

"I was…" She looked down and then across at the dining table. "Maybe you should take a seat."

Her little sister strutted toward the sink. "I can finish the dishes for you."

"Later, Eliza."

"Oh, I won't disturb you."

Tara glared.

Her little sister threw her hands up. "Okay, I'm going to my room. Don't worry, I won't be coming out anytime soon." A pause, then, "I'd go to the library and leave you alone, except I'm grounded." She trudged away, winking at me after she had her back to her sister.

Tara covered her mouth but I couldn't tell if she was concealing a smile or a grimace. I wasn't taking anything for granted, not anymore.

She leaned back against the counter. "Your dad came to see me."

"He what?" Shock rocketing through me, I had no idea what he'd said or the damage he'd caused. I held a hand out, forced myself to get my head together. "I'm not like him."

"I know."

"My father's an asshole."

She folded her arms. "No arguments from me."

I'd be on speaking terms with him as soon as I'd calmed down. He was still my father after all, but things would never be the same between us.

"I don't need him to practice architecture. I'd much rather partner up with Ryan and start from scratch." I stepped closer. "Maybe I went too fast with that idea about buying the bar. Can you forget about that? Because I'm here, Tara, and I'm not going away."

Her lips trembling, she lowered her gaze. Somehow it made me all the more certain I was doing the right thing—in quitting the band, in leaving the touring and the groupies behind, and the weird stalker too.

I was back in Frankston for good and pursuing my dreams and Tara was a part of that. The biggest dream of all.

"There's something I want you to have." I dug out the keys from my pocket and took her hand, then wrapped her fingers around the keys.

She unfurled them. "What's this?"

"The keys to the Thunderbird. It's all yours."

Confusion in her face. "This is your Reverend Horton Heat key ring."

"A great band. I figured you might as well have the key ring too."

She looked up at me, her eyes wide. "But you love the Thunderbird."

"I want you to have it, no matter what."

"I-I'm... This... I can't..."

"You're the one I love, Tara, not the car."

Her mouth fell open, her face frozen. Not the reaction I wanted but I couldn't stop here.

I took her hands into mine, found she was trembling. "Before, I'd asked you to move into my place but you didn't seem wild about that idea. I can move in here. If you'll have me. My place is too big and empty anyway. I don't need a big house. I need you. I want to be with you."

I pressed a gentle kiss to her lips. She didn't respond, didn't kiss me back, didn't push me away either. It wasn't a refusal. Wasn't far from it either. Disappointment flooded me. I'd done this all wrong and gone too fast again.

"I want to be with you," I said.

She bit her lip.

"Will you think about it?"

She nodded.

And I wanted her to say the same words. They didn't come. I swallowed the lump in my throat. I'd had Eliza on my side, done what I could, given a gift that was straight from my heart, the only thing I owned that truly meant something to me.

My throat tightened, my chest ready to cave in. I held her gaze for a moment, looking for a sign, waiting for her to jump into my arms, aching for her to want me in her life.

There was only so much a man could take. I turned and left, closed the door behind me, and walked down the front path. The pearlescent paint shone pale pink and green in the sun, the very sight of the Thunderbird sending a pang through my heart.

Still, it was Tara I wanted, not the car. I hadn't been lying.

Footsteps behind me. I turned. Tara came flying down the front path, hands outstretched as she leapt into my arms and I spun her around. In my arms. Where she was meant to be. My heart swelled.

She placed her hands on my chest. "I've thought about it. The answer is yes, yes, yes, a hundred times yes." On tiptoes, she tilted her head to whisper in my ear, "I love you, Austin."

I grinned, held her gaze. "Well, that's very handy because I love you too."

She took a step back, placed her hands on her hips. "Hey, who said you could lean on my car?" Then more slowly, "This *is* my car, isn't it?"

"The car's all yours and you're all mine."

I cupped her jaw in my hands so I could kiss her slowly and she kissed me back. She snaked her arms around my neck to pull me closer and I held her tight. We fit together so well. This was meant to be.

After a while, she pulled back, a sly smile on her face. "So, ah, how had you been planning on getting back home?"

I grinned. "To tell you the truth, I hadn't thought that bit through properly."

She laughed. "Well, you don't need to worry about that now." Taking my hand into hers, she pulled me back up the front path. "We should go inside. I can show you where the bedroom is."

"I'd like that."

I'd like it very much.

CHAPTER TWENTY

Tara

Austin moved in right away, didn't waste any time since we'd already wasted enough. And now we were moving again—to his place, which would soon be our place.

I couldn't deny that Austin's home was in a much nicer part of town than Grandma's house. The only problem was that it was further from Eliza's school, and that was her problem. She had the Micra now. All she had to do was get her driver's license.

Hands on hips, I admired the new living room. "The club sofa and chairs looked kind of big in the old place. They don't look so big here. There's all this space."

Austin came up behind me, pressed a kiss to my neck. "I love those old leather sofas and wouldn't change them for the world. We can model the room around them, get a rug, maybe a sideboard, fill the place out."

"And make this a home."

"I'm already home." He wrapped his arms around me from behind. "Home is where you are."

I felt so comfortable and everything felt so right. The house may have been huge but to me it felt cozy, snug, and serene. Or it would be after we were done with it.

"Oh my god, Tara, have you seen the size of the bathtub?"

Eliza's voice. I should have known.

I stepped away, kept the exasperation from my voice. "No, but I'm sure you're going to tell me about it."

"It's enormous." Eliza spread her arms. "One of those giant freestanding things in sparkling white. The shower is huge too. The mirror is huge. Everything is huge."

"It's your tub. You can take a bath right now if you like. "

"I can't do that." She looked at me as if I was an idiot. "I'm too busy. I've got to unpack first."

"Yep, you'd better get onto it then," Austin said.

"Oh, sure." Suddenly more serious, she turned away to get back to work. Eliza adored Austin and hung off his every word, which made him my new secret weapon because when he asked her to do something, she did it.

As soon as she left, he took me into his arms. "We need coffee."

I could do with a break from unpacking. "Good idea."

"You might need cake."

My stomach was practically rumbling already. "I might."

"We can go out for coffee. Eliza will be fine on her own. We could bring her back a tub of ice cream from Peppe's."

No matter what we were doing, he always considered Eliza because he knew how important she was to me. Maybe she was a tiny bit important to him too.

He'd already told me he'd take care of her college education but I wasn't quite ready to tell her that yet because I liked the idea of her applying for scholarships. She was a smart girl and might get one.

I took his hand into mine. "I'll drive."

Austin had bought himself a black Audi sedan, which was way too sensible for my liking, so I drove whenever we went anywhere.

He held my hand. "Tonight it'll be just me and you."

I kissed him lightly on the lips. "Me and you. Always."

I hadn't known love could feel so good.

Keep reading for a sneak preview of Book 3

ACKNOWLEDGMENTS

First of all, a big thanks to my very own rock star and in-house consultant, James.

Thanks very much to the people I interviewed, all experts in your particular fields and very patient with my dumb questions—Jenny Kim, Brooke Lundy, Scott Wilson, Brendan Murphy and Jo Taylor. Thanks heaps, guys!

And of course thanks to my fabulous critique partners, Claire, Lorraine, Juanita, Teena and Anna.

ABOUT THE AUTHOR

Susanna Rogers is the author of rock star romances for adults and kick butt books for young adults. Inspired by her very own in-house rock star and years of going to gigs, she penned the Mosh Series after writing and releasing several young adult novels. She's also a kickboxer and dreams of empowering girls and guys around the globe to believe in themselves, to take care and follow their own dreams. She has a soft spot for romantic suspense, also with kick butt heroines, so you never know what might be coming up next.

She would love to hear from you—susannarogers.com.

If you like her books, please post a review on Amazon or Goodreads. She'd like that a lot.

SLASH & BURN
MOSH BOOK 3

CHAPTER ONE

Lachie

Another day, another hangover. A couple of aspirin had taken care of the headache but there was no miracle cure for the nausea and sluggishness. And that was the least of my problems.

At least they'd cranked up the air conditioning at the bar. I loved being back in Nevada. Hated the heat. And I'd always had a soft spot for The Swamp even if it was a dump. Sometimes I still couldn't believe Nick had bought the place.

I leaned back in my chair. "What's taking so long with the renovations?"

He looked up from the other side of the table. "Problems with the planning authority. Austin's handling it."

Austin. Our ex-bass player, also an architect. I gritted my teeth. Better I didn't say anything about that particular subject. It hadn't been long since he'd quit the band and I was still pissed about it.

"We did up the bathrooms already, Lachie," Nick said.

"Yeah, I noticed. It makes going to the john less of a life and death experience."

Nick laughed, glanced down at his phone on the table. "Andrew's nearly here."

I scowled. "Don't know why you made me get up at the crack of dawn for this."

"It's noon, dude." He gave me a concerned look that was very unlike him. "Hey, we don't want to lose another band member."

Which made me think of someone else. The words sent a pang through my heart and I wasn't exactly a pang-in-the-heart kind of guy.

Nick was overreacting, though. They all were. They weren't going to lose me just because a stalker had been sending me Facebook messages. Called herself Angel. And referred to me as her darling. I was not her fucking darling and I had enough shit in my life already.

"This isn't going to work. You're wasting your time." The only reason I was here today was to put an end to this latest idea.

Nick stood. "They're here."

"They?"

He'd told me we were meeting Andrew Shields, head of Shields Security, for a friendly lunch. I knew what friendly meant. Didn't know he was bringing someone with him.

Andrew ushered a young woman ahead of him through the door and strode toward our table. So did she.

This woman was the opposite of Andrew, a big African American guy—and I mean linebacker-sized—with a huge gleaming smile against dark skin.

Whereas she was very much woman-sized and shaped. She'd pulled her light brown hair into a ponytail that showed off her pale skin and gray eyes. No smile. Only composure, loads of composure, practically overflowing with it. Something I should have more of. I made sure my tongue wasn't hanging out of my mouth.

Andrew motioned toward me. "I'd like you to meet Jess Hermann."

I shook her hand, stopped myself from grinning like an idiot, though it was a close thing. "Hi, I'm Lachie Tyler."

"I know. Pleased to meet you." Jess sat beside me, poised and unperturbed.

"Would you like some drinks to start?"

Tara, the bartender or bar manager or whatever she was, appeared out of nowhere the way she often seemed to. She was Austin's girlfriend, which didn't exactly put her in my good books, but I was getting over it.

"Sparkling mineral water would be lovely," Jess said.

Andrew nodded. "Same for me."

Nick agreed. He seemed to be turning over a new leaf or some such crap and had been for a while.

"I'll have the Frankston IPA, thanks," I said, because one beer wouldn't hurt and I refused to bow to the pressure of the non-drinkers.

"The best beer in town." Tara smiled, made me feel as if she was on my side, which was kind of weird.

She came back with the drinks and left menus with us while we went through the usual banter about the band and people we knew. Nick talked about his family because he was in love all over again and couldn't help himself. Jess didn't say much. Not much for her to say when she was with three guys who'd known each other for years.

A waitress came for our food orders. Nick and Andrew ordered stuff that sounded too much like health food for my liking. I stuck with the burger and fries while Jess contemplated the menu, a cute frown forming in her brow.

"The burgers are the best in town," I said. "Flame-grilled on toasted Turkish buns."

She handed back the menu. "You talked me into it."

A girl with an appetite. Not too many of those around, or not in my world anyway.

After the waitress left, Nick finally came out with it. "You know why we're here?"

"Of course I do. And I haven't changed my mind. I don't want this sort of—" I searched for the right word — "intrusion in my life."

"It's for your own safety."

That got my back up. As if he hadn't done any crazy shit and had his share of wild women throwing themselves at him.

He added, "This is coming from the whole band, not just me."

"The whole band? That's only you and Cooper." Our drummer hadn't been able to make it today. "Not a lot of us left."

"And Brett. He was the one who organized this."

Our manager had already spoken to me about this. I might be outnumbered but I wasn't outmaneuvered.

The last couple of messages from the stalker had been increasingly threatening, stuff about how she'd hunt me down if god told her to. It had freaked me out, not that I'd let it show.

I just wanted it all to go away. Maybe the person would get bored, move on, and the problem would disappear. This wasn't a part of my life and couldn't be happening. I mean, it wasn't as if we were One Direction or I was Justin Bieber with thousands of screaming girl fans. We had plenty of followers but they weren't so frenzied and generally knew when to lay off.

"When we're all together we've got security for the band." I spread my arms. "That's fine when we're touring but I've been through this with you. You and Cooper don't have personal bodyguards and I don't want that either. I don't fancy having a team of guys trailing me and watching my every move. I just want to live my life and I've got enough on my plate at the moment."

Nick knew exactly what I was referring to. My dad had gone through bowel cancer years ago and now it had come back with a vengeance, more aggressive, more surprising than the first time, though you'd think we'd have been used to it. Some things you don't get used to.

It felt as if the world was shifting beneath my feet. Maybe that was why I'd taken the news about Austin leaving the band so badly. I swallowed back the pain that had nothing to do with Austin and everything to do with my father.

The conversation slowed as our meals arrived. I'd never felt less like a burger and fries in my life, even though my stomach was telling me I should eat.

The place was bustling, the tables all taken, a wall of noise around us. This wasn't The Swamp that I knew. I used to feel comfortable here.

"Lachie." Jess's voice snapped me back to attention. "I don't know what else you've got going on in your life and that's not really my concern."

I tried to sound casual. "Everyone's got problems."

"But personal security is our business and I think your

friend has a point."

"That's what I've been trying to tell you, dude," Nick said. "It's why Jess is here."

Because she was some sort of security guard? Was that what he meant?

Maybe it should have sunk in earlier but I'd been too taken by the sight of her and my head was still foggy from last night's booze.

I turned to her. "So you work for Andrew?"

"That's right."

"You don't exactly look the part." Understatement of the year.

Andrew leaned forward. "That's why she's perfect for the job. She's smart, anticipates problems, and doesn't hesitate to call for help if she needs it. Above all, she blends in. No one is going to look at her and automatically think she's your bodyguard, and that gives her one up on them."

I glanced at Jess, tried not to stare too much. I couldn't imagine in what universe he thought this young woman might 'blend in' because, to me, she had a serenity and a presence that made her stand out.

I ate a few of the fries on my plate. Not so bad. Pretty damn good, in fact.

Andrew continued, "You don't want someone who'll intrude on your life or cramp your style? Not a problem. Jess is very good at staying in the background but she'll be there if and when you need her."

I raised my eyebrows. "Do you really think I'll need her?"

"What do *you* think?"

I hated it when people threw my own questions back

at me, especially when I was doing such a good job of avoiding the answers myself.

I turned to Jess. "Do you mind if I ask how old you are?"

"Twenty-five."

Same as me. "And how long have you been doing—" I waved my hand —"this?"

"Several years, on and off, but I've been training a lot longer than that."

"Yeah, what do you do?"

"I'm a kickboxer. Started when I was fourteen and fell in love with it." The faraway smile on her face told me she wasn't kidding.

"So you can pack a punch? Have you ever had to use this against someone?"

"I've done my share of door work at pubs and clubs, and I've been in a couple of altercations when I absolutely couldn't help it, but that's the whole point. Whenever possible, you want to avoid things getting to that stage."

"I wouldn't mind seeing you in action." It simply didn't gel with me that this slender female in jeans and a white T-shirt could be some sort of fighting machine. "And guns? I presume you guys carry?"

"When necessary, yes, but my best weapon is my brain."

I whooped with laughter, then looked around to see no one else was laughing.

Jess gave me a look so scary it shut me up quick and made me think Andrew might be right about her.

Nick raised his eyebrows. "Haven't you noticed the way our security guys work when we're at a concert or making an appearance somewhere?"

I shrugged. "What?"

"They're the reason we don't run into any problems. Because they have a sense for what's coming, get in early, and stop bad shit from happening."

I hated it when Nick was a smart ass. Hated it when he was right too.

"So you've been talking to Andrew?" I raised my eyebrows. "You got this from him?"

"Actually," Andrew said, "he's been *listening* to me."

And I wasn't. I got the message.

Problem was, I didn't want to listen. It was easier to hide my head in the sand and pretend everything was fine.

Still, a part of me had a horrible feeling that this thing with the stalker was one of those issues that was going to get bigger before it went away. Much bigger. It'd been eating away at me for a while.

Nick leaned forward. "Look, we don't want you to end up like John Lennon. We want to avoid that at all costs."

I swallowed. "Hey, I'd rather be alive than be a legend."

"There, you've said it. We'd rather you stayed alive too, Lachie."

Alive…

My dad was teaching me the value of life every day, the importance of being with the people who mattered, and how you should make the most of every day. Instead, I was wasting my days being hungover and my nights being drunk.

I held a hand out. "I'll think about it. That's all I'm saying for now."

Nick started to say something but I told him we should eat and finished off the rest of my burger. My stomach felt a lot better after it had something in it that wasn't liquid.

We continued with some polite conversation, which made me suspicious because Nick didn't do 'polite'.

He cleared his throat. "One more thing."

"What?"

"You need someone with you twenty-four-seven."

"Huh? But that'd mean someone moving in with me."

Surely he didn't mean Jess. He couldn't be serious. I'd never lived with someone and wasn't that sort of guy. For one thing, the opportunity had never come up because I'd been too young when I'd been dating my one long-term girlfriend, and now I specialized in the short-term. I didn't want someone who was a permanent fixture at my place.

Nick wasn't done yet. "You need someone with you all the time, dude. You drink a lot and then you don't always know what you're doing."

A hand on my chest. "*I* drink a lot? That's rich coming from you."

"You're so busy having a good time that you're not looking out for anything else. If something bad happened, you wouldn't even see it coming."

I scowled. "When did you get to be so mature and responsible?" I held a hand out. "Don't answer that."

"Andrew explained this stuff to me. They call this close protection. *Close.* You need someone to move in and keep an eye on you."

"Well, that could be tricky. It might really cramp my style."

Jess scraped her chair back. "Honestly, that's the last thing you should be worried about."

My jaw tight, I couldn't bring myself to look at her,

couldn't imagine her moving in with me, not in the way they meant. Because they weren't talking about her jumping into bed with me. That was something I had no problem imagining. They were talking about her shifting into the spare room and overseeing my every movement, and that was just downright weird.

"Think about it, Lachie." Andrew leaned forward, smirking. "Hey, would you like me to move in with you instead, buddy?"

He and Nick laughed. Jess smiled wanly, going along with it.

That's when it hit me. They were serious.